D1319870

Nantucket Summer

Also by Phyllis Green

The Fastest Quitter in Town

Nantucket Summer

by
Phyllis Green

publishers since 1798

THOMAS NELSON INC.
NASHVILLE / NEW YORK

All rights reserved under International and Pan-American Conventions. Published in Nashville, Tennessee, by Thomas Nelson Inc., and simultaneously in Don Mills, Ontario, by Thomas Nelson & Sons (Canada) Limited. Manufactured in the United States of America.

First edition

Library of Congress Cataloging in Publication Data

Green, Phyllis.
  Nantucket summer.
  SUMMARY: Thirteen-year-old A.D. unwillingly accepts a summer babysitting job on Nantucket Island and finds it far more pleasurable than she expected even though she must cope with her employer's mental problems and a ghostly visitor.
  [1. Nantucket, Massachusetts—Fiction] I. Title.
PZ7.G82615Nan [Fic] 74–10276
ISBN 0–8407–6403–0

For my husband
Bob

Nantucket Summer

Chapter One

Adriana dialed her home number. She listened as the phone rang once, twice, three times. She looked nervously around the Cramers' kitchen. Four, five. Where was her mother? She brushed her hair out of her eyes and back over her shoulder. Six. *Click*.

"Uh-uh."

"Mother, what a way to answer. How do you know it's going to be me?"

"A.D., you've called six times tonight. And the last time was five minutes ago."

"Mother, I don't like this baby-sitting job. I told you I wouldn't. We made a bargain. You said if I didn't like baby-sitting, I wouldn't have to do it. Well, I don't like it."

"All right, you'll never have to sit again. But you don't stop in the middle of a job, either."

"Mother, this house creaks."

"Is Stephanie all right?"

"I haven't even seen her. She was already sleeping

when I got here. There's nothing to do. I hate it. I'm scared. I still need a baby-sitter myself. What am I doing over here a thousand miles from home?"

"You're next door."

"That isn't the point. When this house creaks, I'm a thousand miles away. Why did you have to get me this job in the creakiest house in town?"

"Honey, I'm here if you need me. I have to get back to my article."

"Mother, if I know you, you are sitting there this minute writing an article entitled 'How Your Teen Can Enjoy Baby-sitting Even Though She Still Sucks Her Thumb' or 'The Night I Hung Up the Phone While My Baby-sitting Teen Got Murdered.' "

"No, it's called 'Sex, How Far Should You Go?' "

"Mother!"

"Darling, I've really got to get back to it."

"Mother, will you please consider writing under a pseudonym before I die from embarrassment?"

Adriana hung up the phone, and then she regretted it. She realized she had wanted to talk more with her mother about the dog, Harold Poopsie, and the signs in the big bedroom.

As soon as the Cramers had left, the beagle, Harold Poopsie, ran upstairs. She had followed him to take a peek at the little girl, Stephanie. She had never been upstairs at the Cramers', so when Harold Poopsie went into a bedroom, she did too, thinking it was Stephanie's room. She turned on the light in time to see Harold Poopsie jump on the big bed, raise his back leg, and pee on the pillows. She ran to chase him off.

That was when she saw the signs. They were huge

lettered posters on two walls of the master bedroom: big black letters on a stark-white background, and they sort of whirled around and made her dizzy like op art. But they were obviously homemade signs.

"I am Cynthia Cramer," they said. "I live in Livonia, Michigan. I shop at Hudson's Westland, Crowley's Livonia Mall, and Saks and Bonwits in Troy. My friends are Ann Prushtak, writer, Beverly Kisco, bridge player."

One of the signs told who her doctors were. One said, "I have a baby girl, Stephanie. She is two years old." Then it told what Stephanie liked to eat, when she napped, and so on.

Reading the signs gave Adriana a creepy feeling. She picked up the wet pillows and took them down to the clothes dryer. They came out dry, but smelly. What she had meant to ask her mother was should she wash the pillows? Was she responsible for what Harold Poopsie did, or was she just responsible for Stephanie? She decided to put the smelly pillows back on the bed and not to look at the signs when she did it.

Adriana had put off baby-sitting as long as possible. All the neighbors had started asking her when she was twelve.

"Grrrr," she would roar like a lion. "I don't like those grimy little kids with their ears full of wax and green snot dripping out of their noses."

"All girls baby-sit," her mother would say, typing as she spoke.

"All but one."

"You'll change your mind next year when you hit thirteen. You'll like the money." Her mother stopped typing long enough to jot down in her Future Notebook an article she wanted to write called "Baby-sitting—the Money's Fine."

Adriana checked the bolts on the front and back doors again. She stared at the basement door, which held behind it the hiding place of a strange creaking.

"They couldn't pay me a thousand dollars to do this again. Even their color TV is out of order. Maybe I should go look at Stephanie to see if she's breathing."

She walked up the stairs, and the beagle wanted to follow her.

"Down, down, Harold Poopsie. Heel. Down. Stay. I don't need any more of your cute little tricks upstairs."

He finally sat down at the bottom of the steps, looking dejected.

She found the baby's room and switched on the light. She tiptoed toward the crib and had to smile when she saw the bundle in the bed.

Little Stephanie was sleeping on her stomach with her bottom sticking up in the air. She had uncovered herself. A.D. gently pulled the soft pink cover over her and lightly tucked it in around Stephanie's shoulders. The little girl slept on while A.D. watched her.

"You're really beautiful," she whispered. "When I came home from school yesterday and you turned the garden hose on me, I had no idea you were such a beautiful little girl. You're almost as pretty as my doll Dorothy."

A.D. lightly brushed a curl away from near Stephanie's eye.

12

"I can see you're really worried about those old creaks. Well, I won't let them get you."

She tiptoed out of the room, turned off the light, and went downstairs. The beagle was delighted to see her and jumped up on her lap as soon as she sat down on the sofa. There was nothing to do but pet it.

When the Cramers came home, they were filled with praise for her. What a fine job she had done! Had the baby wakened? No! Well, it proved she was an excellent baby-sitter.

It did? A.D. put the two dollars in her purse and insisted that Mr. Cramer didn't have to walk her home. "I'll just run across the grass," she said.

She found her mother typing at the dining-room table.

"Mother, don't you think it's weird about the signs?"

"Oh, they're probably fun posters."

"How could anybody call a dog Harold Poopsie!"

"Cynthia Cramer is a very nice person."

"I think so too, Mother. I think she's beautiful, sort of fragile looking, like a delicate Guinevere."

"There's some chocolate cake left."

Adriana wandered into the kitchen. She cut a piece of cake and was stuffing it into her mouth when her father popped his head in, saying, "Home already, A.D.?"

"Hi, Daddy," she mumbled through the cake.

"Mostly cloudy skies tomorrow with a chance of rain likely in the early morning, late afternoon, or evening. Highs will be sixty-eight to seventy with overnight lows of fifty to fifty-four. Winds southeasterly. One year ago the high was sixty-five, the low fifty-two."

"Thanks, Daddy, I was worried about it. How is the air traffic over Chicago?"

Her father relighted his pipe. "Very heavy. Don't fly into Chicago this time of night if you can help it."

She put her knife and dish in the sink. "Okay. Good night, Daddy." She hugged him.

"Off to bed?" he asked.

"Are you kidding? I have tons of homework." She went up to her room.

When she had finished with her books, almost two hours later, Adriana flopped into bed.

"Oh, Dorothy," she whispered to the doll she slept with, "I was baby-sitting tonight in the creakiest house. Oh, Dorothy, I just hope you never have to baby-sit."

The doll looked straight up at the ceiling as she always did. A.D. touched the chipped mark on the doll's forehead.

"Close your eyes, Dorothy." She pulled down the doll's eyelids. Then she closed her own eyes and went to sleep.

Chapter Two

Adriana knew, when she heard her mother calling her, that it was much too early. She had not slept nearly enough. It seemed this year of her life she could easily sleep till noon every day.

She groaned and opened her eyes. The huge poster on the wall with its big black letters seemed to jump into her bed. She sat up, pulling the covers around her, and read it.

> My name is A. D. Prushtak.
> I think I am so beautiful.
> I think I am so great.
> I will be the only bride in history
> to take a doll with me on my honeymoon.
> I love Eric Peatman.

She jumped out of bed and tore it off her wall. "Mother! Do you know what Brian did?"

She ran into Brian's room, tearing the poster into bits and throwing them on his bed, on his desk, into his closet. She found him hiding behind the door, still in his red-and-white-striped pajamas. He was giggling.

"Do you want to know what happens to misguided eleven-year-olds? People congregate in cemeteries and say nice things about them. And just for the record, I loathe Eric Peatman. And that puts him one level above you."

She ran out of his room and down to the kitchen.

"Mother, do you have to tell Brian everything? Do you know what he did?"

Her mother was standing by the stove, waiting for the teakettle to whistle.

"I thought your poster was rather cute. He made one for Daddy and me too. Mine said some unfounded thing about how my fat had settled into my seat from sitting around typing all day. But your father's was quite succinct, an inaccurate weather report."

"Those are funny, but I don't think mine was. I guess I feel particularly vulnerable about Dorothy. All the girls at school got rid of their dolls long ago. But I just can't bear to part with Dorothy."

"Don't worry about it, darling. You're just a slow starter."

"All the girls in my class have been wearing bras since the sixth grade. I shouldn't even be wearing this training thing. It keeps slipping up around my neck."

Her father came into the kitchen, carrying his brief-case.

"Time to go to work, Dad?" A.D. asked.

The teakettle whistled as his wife kissed him. "Have a good day, dear," she said.

He looked at his watch. "Well, I'm off. The pollution index is fifty-six. Take care."

Adriana looked at the clock. "Mother, why do you get me up in the middle of the night to go to school? I could have slept for nine more minutes."

On the way home from school that afternoon, A.D. walked with her good friend Linda.

"Just look at these books!" A.D. held the six books up to Linda's face. "If they don't stop giving me so much homework, I'll end up being the smartest kid in the school."

"I had two study halls today," Linda said.

"You must be the principal's long-lost daughter."

"I read your mother's article."

"Was it yukky?"

"All the boys were teasing Eric Peatman about it."

"I loathe Eric Peatman. What was the article?"

"It was called 'A Mother's Private Conversations with Her Daughter.' Telling her about the birds and the bees."

"Yuk. My mother fabricates those articles. We've never had a talk about anything. I still believe in the stork."

"The boys think you know all about it. That's why they were teasing Eric."

"You know, I really do loathe him. My mother is always writing stories where the heroine loathes the boy, but at the end of the story she winds up going to

17

the dance with him. I say it's a good thing she calls it fiction because nothing could be further from the truth. When I say I loathe Eric Peatman, you can believe it."

"I have to wash my hair today. It feels like it's walking home three blocks behind me."

"Oh, Linda, look! There's the little girl I baby-sat last night. Isn't she cute? Look, she's making mud pies. Hi, Stephanie! Here she comes. No, Stephanie, don't touch me. I have on a new—*stop it*—skirt. Linda, should I let the mud dry before I try to clean my skirt?"

Chapter Three

The next Saturday A.D. woke up and found that her doll Dorothy had fallen out of bed.

"Dorothy, this bed isn't big enough for both of us. You've got to go."

A.D.'s long brown hair had tangled in the night and hung down over her face. She tucked it back behind her ears, picked up the doll, and opened its eyes.

"Now don't argue. I know you've been around here a long time. Mother says I got you when I was three, so that's ten years. Ten years, Dorothy. What do you think of that?"

She straightened the doll's dress. It had become yellowed. When she got the doll the dress had been white.

"What are you doing hanging around with a teenager anyhow? What you need is a little girl who will comb your curls and feed you. It's a disgrace. I haven't given you a tea party for years. All we get is a little talk now and then. Wouldn't you like to have more fun?"

She turned the doll around and curled its blond fuzzy hair around her second finger.

"Now don't even think about crying, Dorothy. I won't allow it. You must think of it this way. It happens to all girls and their dolls. All my friends have given up their dolls long ago. Yes, really. You shouldn't be shocked."

She put the doll on her pillow and leaned on her elbows to continue the conversation. The doll stared at the ceiling.

"I think we'll have a garage sale. Brian can help. We'll clean out lots of toys and find new homes for all of you. You, Dorothy, of course, will be the star of the garage sale. All the little girls in the neighborhood will be fighting for the right to buy you. What do you think, Dorothy?"

A.D. looked at the doll. She touched the chipped mark on the doll's forehead.

"I'll put a Band-Aid on that. Dorothy, will you please quit staring at the ceiling and tell me what you think? Wait, I'll go ask Brian if he wants to help. Now don't go away. I'll be right back. Brian!"

She found her brother watching television cartoons in the family room.

"Brian, do you want to have a garage sale with me? Let's sell all our toys. It's my idea, so I'll get sixty percent of the cash and you forty percent. Brian? Have you heard anything I said? Brian? Okay, chiseler, we'll divide the money fifty-fifty."

Brian twitched the freckles on his nose.

"Brian, what do you want—seventy-five percent?"

He turned to her. "Huh?" he said, then turned back to the television.

"Brian! If you'd concentrate on your fractions the way you concentrate on the cartoons, you wouldn't be in such trouble in math all the time. I want you to have a garage sale with me."

"When the cartoons are over."

"Of course. I have lots to do. I'll start sorting and pricing the toys, and when your show is over, you write out the invitations and deliver them. Brian? Did you hear me?"

He nodded but did not take his eyes from the set.

A.D. went to get dressed.

Later, in the basement, she stood looking at the toys like a farmer surveying his fields. The basement was an acre of toys. Six pink plastic clothes baskets, overflowing. Cardboard boxes of toys. Bookcases of toys. An antique cradle bursting with dolls. A.D. picked up a talking Barbie doll that was unclothed and had an arm missing.

"I remember you. I got you in a trade for the Stacey with one leg. But where did the rest of this stuff come from? There's a fortune to be made here. Brian and I will end up the day as millionaires."

She began to write up price tags and tape them on the toys. She sorted the broken toys together and printed a sign: BUY ONE TOY, GET A BROKEN TOY FREE.

She marked most of the toys 5¢, some 10¢, a few 25¢, some 1¢. She began to enjoy finding old toys that had been hidden at the bottom of the clothes baskets. It was like seeing a forgotten friend and getting reacquainted. Some of the rediscovered things were hard to part with. An old Silly Putty ball. A three-little-pigs pull-me toy. A pink talking telephone. She felt as if she were selling her whole lifetime.

"These things have all been part of my childhood. I feel so old. I am older today than I've ever been. And that's frightening."

Brian came down to help carry the toys up to the garage.

"Did you deliver the notices about the sale?" A.D. asked.

"Yeah. Is two o'clock okay? That's what I put on. Will we be ready by then? What a mess."

"Two o'clock! You must think I have six hands." She threw up two of her hands in despair.

Brian looked at the toys and the price tags. "How come everything of mine is for one cent and your stuff is ten and twenty-five cents?"

"Because boys' toys are dopey. If we get even one cent, I'll faint. We'll probably have to give them away."

Brian kicked her in the shin and then carried a load of toys up to the garage.

She called after him. "You're misguided, Brian."

At two o'clock they were set up in the garage waiting for their first customer. A large sign out front said GARAGE SALE HERE in big red letters. A.D. admitted to herself that Brian really could be an artist. He had made a gorgeous sign and great invitations.

The toys were displayed on card tables. Dorothy lay in a beautiful white doll's bed, a red-and-white-checked doll blanket covering her. Her tape said SPECIAL PRICE, ASK THE CASHIER.

"How much are you selling Dorothy for?" Brian asked.

"Do you want to buy her?"

"Good grief, Charlie Brown, are you kidding?"

"I'll be glad to discuss the price with prospective customers," A.D. said. "Why don't you look down the block? See if anyone's coming."

Brian saw two girls coming up the street. They looked as if they were each clutching a fistful of money. He signaled for them to hurry up. While these girls looked over the items, a brother and sister came by and then three boys from Brian's class at school.

A.D. was soon busy making change. The children carried out handfuls of toys they had bought and the broken ones they had gotten for free. Some went home for more money. At one point in the afternoon there were so many children in the garage that there was a waiting line to get in.

At three thirty all of Brian's toys (which sold for a penny) were gone. By four, just a few toys were left, mostly the ones marked 25¢. And Dorothy. She had not been sold.

"Let's mark these prices down and get it over with," Brian said. "I want to play baseball with Carl and Joey."

"Is three cents okay?" A.D. asked.

Brian held up Dorothy. "Last chance to get this fabulous doll for three cents."

A.D. screamed and snatched Dorothy out of his hand. "Not Dorothy. The other things are three cents."

23

"Well, how much is Dorothy?" Brian asked.

"I'm not marking her down."

"Well, how much is she?" he insisted.

A.D. wished she could drop in a hole. "Well," she said, drawing the word to three syllables, "fifty-seven."

"Fifty-seven cents? That's too much for that old thing."

A.D. took a deep breath and looked straight into his green eyes. "Fifty-seven dollars," she said.

Brian's mouth popped open as if someone had told him his foot was on fire. "Fifty-seven *dollars?*" he repeated.

"Don't tell me you won't be glad to take your half if we sell her." A.D. turned away from him and flipped her hair over her shoulder.

"That does it. I'm going to play baseball." He ran out of the garage.

A.D. started to yell "Wait," but he was running too fast. She decided it was just as well. Everything was almost sold. She would finish up, then divide the money with him fifty-fifty. From the looks of the cash box, they would each get three or four dollars. It had been a successful garage sale, and, best of all, she still had Dorothy.

Chapter Four

Several weeks later Cynthia Cramer stepped out on her porch and called to Adriana as she was walking home from school. Mrs. Cramer looked small alone on the porch, and even though it was four thirty in the afternoon, she had on a terry-cloth bathrobe of a soft-yellow color that matched her hair.

A.D. thought at first that Mrs. Cramer was sick and was calling her to help with baby Stephanie. She gulped, then stood paralyzed. She *couldn't* baby-sit now. She had promised Linda she'd go over to her house and work on their science project, red-eyed fruit flies.

Mrs. Cramer smiled. She was so pretty.

"Could you spare five minutes? I want to ask you something," she called.

A.D. walked toward the porch to say she really couldn't. She held out the jar of fruit flies in front of her to prove her excuse was valid. But as she got closer, she saw the dark shadows under Mrs. Cramer's eyes and the pink rims around them. They looked just the way A.D.'s did when she'd been crying. And the lids were puffing out. A.D. knew the feeling.

"Of course I have five minutes!" she said, smiling in what she hoped was a contagious way.

She ran up on the porch. Mrs. Cramer held open the door for her, and she walked inside. She wondered why Mrs. Cramer had been crying, and at the same time she hoped she wouldn't find out. Sadness had a way of creeping up on A.D. If she heard about someone dying, someone she didn't even know, she would start to cry. She cried her way through most books and movies. Her mother told her that when she was small, she had even cried while watching television cartoons.

A.D. and Mrs. Cramer stood in the entry hall, awkwardly looking at each other. Finally, Mrs. Cramer said, "Let me make you some iced tea." She turned and walked to the back of the house where the kitchen was.

A.D. called, "Really I can't." She said it in a helpless way, a way in which she needed to be coaxed. But Mrs. Cramer didn't coax her, or perhaps she didn't hear her. A.D. reclutched her books and science jar and walked into the kitchen.

Mrs. Cramer handed her the glass of iced tea, saying, "Nantucket is the most beautiful island in the world. I want to go there this summer, and I want you to go with me as Stephanie's baby-sitter. Mr. Cramer will come for weekends with us. I can pay you thirty dollars a week. Can you go?"

"What?" said A.D. She put her books and jar of fruit flies on the counter. She picked up the iced tea and sipped it. "What did you say?"

Mrs. Cramer went into the dining room and came back with her hands full of pamphlets.

26

"This is Nantucket," she said, thrusting the pamphlets on A.D. "Come on. We'll sit at the kitchen table. I want to look at the pictures with you."

They moved to the table. A.D. picked up the top pamphlet and looked at a picture of gray-shingled houses with white shutters, roses growing all over the roofs.

"Do the houses really look like this? They're so quaint," A.D. said.

Mrs. Cramer smiled. "Aren't they lovely? The whole island is quaint. The shingles aren't painted gray. They get that color from the rain and wind and sun. I think it is the loveliest place. I used to go every summer when I was young. We stayed at my aunt's cottage on a high hill overlooking the sea. Now it's my house, and I want to go back."

The patio door opened, and Stephanie came in from the backyard, where she had been playing.

"Cookie," she said.

Her mother got up and gave her one. "Just one," she said.

"Hi, Stephanie," A.D. said.

Stephanie stared at her and bit into the cookie.

"Now this is the downtown area," Mrs. Cramer said, pointing to the map. "And there's the new wharf. We'll walk out on it and look at the yachts and sailboats moored there. The shops—"

Stephanie ate her cookie, getting most of the crumbs on the kitchen linoleum. Then she stepped on the crumbs and walked over to the counter. She pulled down one of A.D.'s books and the rest clattered after it onto the floor.

A.D. wanted to pick up the books, but she hated to interrupt Mrs. Cramer.

". . . if you like to bicycle, we'll take your bicycle along in the back of the station wagon. I'll buy a baby seat so Stephanie can ride with you. Nantucket is a marvelous place to bicycle. I might even buy one. I suppose I can still balance." She laughed.

"Uh—pardon me, Mrs. Cramer. Stephanie's taking my jar of fruit flies," A.D. interrupted.

"Be careful with them, Stephanie." Mrs. Cramer turned her head slightly as she called, but then her interest was again caught up in the pamphlets. "I wonder if the house has changed. Sometimes what you remember as a child is not nearly so big when you see it as an adult. I remember it as a big house. I wonder if it is."

"Stephanie, please put my bug jar back on the counter," A.D. pleaded. She looked to Mrs. Cramer for help. "It's my science project."

"Now this is the ferryboat," Mrs. Cramer said, pointing to another pamphlet. "I'll drive the car right onto this boat. Then we can get out and walk around, even eat on the boat. It's a three-hour boat ride. Nantucket is thirty miles out to sea."

"I get seasick," A.D. whispered.

"And we're not far from either the Jetties Beach or the Children's Beach. You and Stephanie can go there every day. See, on the map."

A.D. stood up. "Mrs. Cramer, it sure looks nice. It's a pretty place. But I'll have to ask my mother. Can I let you know later?"

"Take the pamphlets. Study them. It will be a wonderful opportunity." She looked A.D. straight in the eye. Her pale-blue eyes were moist and sort of desperate looking. "I'm counting on you, Adriana. Mr. Cramer says I can't take Stephanie unless I have a baby-sitter for her. Please say yes. Please, for me."

A.D. looked away and picked up her books. She put the Nantucket pamphlets in her ecology notebook.

"I'll have to see what my mom says," she repeated, not really looking at Mrs. Cramer, but sort of gazing at her left ear. "Where did Stephanie take my jar of fruit flies?"

Stephanie came back into the kitchen and handed A.D. the jar. A.D. looked at it. The lid was on, but the jar was empty.

"What did you do with my fruit flies?"

Stephanie threw her hands into the air. "Bugs," she said.

A.D. looked up. The high cupboards and the ceiling were dotted with her science project. Hundreds of popping red eyes were staring down at her. She wanted to die. She at least wanted to faint. Since neither of those things happened, she felt she should apologize to Mrs. Cramer for infesting her home with red-eyed fruit flies. When she looked at her, however, she could see that Mrs. Cramer hadn't even seen or heard. She was smiling as if she were in a strange wonderful dream. Mrs. Cramer was already in Nantucket.

A.D. said good-bye and left the house, determined not to go summering with Mrs. Cramer and Stephanie.

Chapter Five

She ran in the front door, tossed her books and empty science jar in the recliner chair, and threw herself on the plaid davenport. She landed on her back and left her legs and arms sticking straight up.

"Brian, guess what I am! Brian! Are you home?"

No one answered.

"Brian, come see the dead bird."

She sat up and kicked off her shoes. She went into the kitchen and dialed Linda's number.

"Linda, you'll never believe what happened to my fruit flies. Mr. Jacobs is going to kill me. Stephanie, that little girl next door, opened the lid. They're flying all over her house. Linda, I *know* Mr. Jacobs will kill me. How are your fruit flies doing? . . . Ha, ha. . . . Linda— look, I won't bother coming over. I have to talk to my mother, but help me tomorrow with Mr. Jacobs. 'Bye."

She opened the refrigerator, cut a piece of cake, and poured herself a glass of milk.

"Boy, what a day. Some really weird lady wants me to baby-sit her really weird kid in a faraway place, and nobody is home to tell me I can't go."

She went to the bookcase in the family room and took up the large atlas in her arms. She laid it on the kitchen table and paged through to a map of the United States. She studied it. She heard a car drive into the garage. Her mother came in through the mud room.

"Hi, honey," she said, setting a bag of groceries on the map.

"Mother, I'm reading the atlas."

Her mother picked up the bag and set it on the counter. "Sorry, love."

"Mother, do you know how far Massachusetts is from Michigan?"

"A.D., did you clean your room yet?"

"I've been offered this job, but I don't think you'll want me to go so far away."

"You mean Cynthia's spoken to you already about Nantucket?"

"You *knew?*"

"Yes. She mentioned it a couple of days ago. Honey, put this toothpaste and soap on the stairs, will you, and take it up when you go to clean your room. I said, 'Cynthia, thirty dollars a week is too much to offer a thirteen-year-old on her first job.' But she says it's the going rate."

"You don't want me to go, do you, Mother? All that way? Look at the map."

"Honey, you're taller than I am. Put this coffee

can up there, will you? It will be a wonderful vacation for you. Not many girls get such an opportunity."

"I think that little kid hates me. She does things."

"When I saw all those pamphlets, I wished I were going."

"There's this boat. And it's at least a three-hour trip. You know how seasick I get."

Her mother folded the bag and put it in a drawer. She turned to A.D. "Honey, I didn't know you were ever in a boat."

"Well, I think I'd be seasick. It's the same thing, isn't it? See, I'd probably talk myself into it."

"Honey, go clean your room. We'll talk to Daddy at dinner."

A.D. hovered around the front door as it neared her father's getting-home time. She pounced on him when the door opened.

"Daddy! My first love! I thought you'd never get home," she cooed.

He set his briefcase under the hall table. "It was supposed to rain this afternoon. I can't understand what happened."

She took his raincoat and hung it in the closet. She put his big black umbrella in the rack. "Daddy, what would you do here without me?" she asked.

"Couldn't do without you, my dear," he said, kissing her forehead. He went into the kitchen and greeted his wife. "I was supposed to get wet feet today." He laughed. He rubbed his stomach and looked in the oven door to see what was cooking.

At dinner A.D. thought they'd never get around to discussing her and the Cramers and Nantucket.

Mrs. Prushtak dished out seconds to her husband. "Do you want more?" she asked Brian.

Brian wrinkled up his face. "What is it? I'd give anything for a hot dog."

"That's what Nantucket looks like," A.D. said, almost bursting to get on the subject. "A hot dog. On the map. A little hot dog off the coast of Cape Cod."

Her mother tried to make a sign to her. "I thought we'd wait till Daddy finished his dinner," she said, with a meaningful look.

"But I don't want to go," A.D. said.

"Where don't you want to go?" her father asked.

"Nantucket. Mrs. Cramer wants me to baby-sit Stephanie all summer."

"Various commercial airlines serve Nantucket. On a year-round basis you can fly in and out of Nantucket to New York, Boston, Hyannis, and New Bedford."

A.D. sighed deeply. "Daddy, you sound like a travel folder."

His eyebrows went up. "Have you got any? I love to read them. It'll keep me busy all night." She handed him the pamphlets, and he eagerly scanned them.

"Sounds fine," he said. "Sounds like a great place. I'll check my almanacs tonight and let you know what the weather will be like."

He was really enthusiastic. A.D. felt as if a trap were closing in on her. She kept saying, in every way she knew, that she didn't want to go, but nobody was listening. She stood up to go to her room, and the tears

33

burst out of her eyes before she got to the door. She was so embarrassed for them to see her crying that she shouted to the chandelier above the table, "I'm not going anywhere with that crazy lady and her miserable kid."

She ran to the stairs. Through her sobs she could hear her father clicking his tongue.

"Well," he said, "as Elmer Woodring says, 'If a teenager thinks you're crazy, you're all right in my book.' "

A.D. fell onto her bed, feeling abused. She hugged Dorothy and splashed her face with tears.

"Oh, Dorothy," she said, "I don't know what's going to happen. There are only two more weeks of school before summer vacation. I don't want to go. But I'll tell you one thing: if I have to go to Nantucket, you do too."

Chapter Six

Her bike and bags were all packed. Dorothy was in the tote bag she clutched in her shaking hand. A.D. and her family were standing around the Cramers' yellow station wagon. Mrs. Cramer, Stephanie, and Harold Poopsie were in the car.

She hugged her mother. "Are you sure you want me to go?"

Her mother looked as though she might cry. "I'm not sure, now that it's time. I'll miss you, darling. Have a wonderful summer. Be careful. Be good."

"Don't worry, Mother," Brian said. "A.D. won't take drugs. She won't drink. She won't neck. She won't pet. She'll just go all the way."

A.D. stuck her tongue out at him and got into the car. She sat in back, next to Stephanie in her car seat. Harold Poopsie sat up front with Mrs. Cramer.

A.D. blew her mother and father kisses out the open window. "Daddy, don't you have anything special to tell me?" she asked.

"A cloudless day. Beautiful for flying," he said.

"But we're driving," Mrs. Cramer said, smiling.

"Good for that too," he said. He winked at A.D. "I love you, darling. We all do."

"Not me," Brian said.

Mrs. Cramer started the car. They were on their way. A.D. waved and kept waving long after she couldn't see them.

"We can go two ways," Mrs. Cramer explained, "the Ohio Turnpike or through Canada. Let's go one way and come home the other."

"Okay."

Soon they were out of Michigan and into Ohio. When they passed Exit 7 on the Ohio Turnpike, A.D. said, "This is as far as I've been. We come to Cedar Point every summer. Now everything is new. I've never been east."

"I think you'll like it," Mrs. Cramer said.

A.D. thought perhaps the long ride was going to be pleasant after all. Mrs. Cramer was in a happy mood and had been talking and laughing ever since they left Livonia. She really was excited about Nantucket. Her excitement was spreading, and A.D. was beginning to look forward to it too.

"I made reservations for us at a motel in Syracuse, New York, for tonight," Mrs. Cramer said. "Tomorrow we'll get up early, in time to get to Woods Hole to catch the two o'clock boat. We have reservations for our car on that boat."

"I think it's going to be fun," A.D. said.

Mrs. Cramer smiled. She was so happy. "Of course it is!"

They stopped for lunch; then back in the car Stephanie took a nap. They were in New York State, on the Thruway, driving past Buffalo.

"We used to live in Buffalo," Mrs. Cramer said. "That was our third move. I still have some friends there that I write Christmas cards to, but right now I can't think of their names."

"You've lived in lots of places, haven't you?" A.D. asked.

Mrs. Cramer sighed. "We have lived in fifteen cities all over the country in twenty-one years of marriage."

"Wow."

"And really, Jerry tells me that's not unusual. Lots of men in the company have moved more than that. But I can't take it any longer. I have these terrible nightmares. I call them my lost-friendship nightmares. I wake up sweating. 'Why don't we ever see Lee and George anymore?' I say to Jerry. He'll say, 'Lee and George live in Dallas.' You see, in my nightmares, I forget. I don't know where we live. I honestly want to shop at I. Magnin's, but I wake up in Livonia, and I. Magnin's is in San Francisco. Jerry constantly has to remind me where we are and who our friends are. That's why I get so uptight sometimes. That's why he was thrilled I could go to Nantucket for the summer. Back to childhood. Neutral ground. No sweaty nightmares, that sort of thing. Do you possibly understand any of this?" she asked lightly, laughing.

"I've always lived around Detroit. I think it would be fun to move," A.D. said.

"Well, you can move or you can be gypsies. We're

37

gypsies. The company created our breed. The corporate gypsy."

"Where else have you lived?"

"We *haven't* lived in Atlanta or Portland. Every place else, we've lived."

"Gee."

Mrs. Cramer gave back the map to A.D. "Check the map, please, Adriana. See how far to Syracuse now. I'll be glad to stop driving. My back is killing me."

A.D. reported the mileage yet to go. She felt good, good to be traveling and seeing new things, good to be caring for little Stephanie, who had fallen into a nap so easily, good to be treated like an adult by Mrs. Cramer. She didn't know why she had ever hesitated about the summer. It was going to be a wonderful summer. She just knew it.

They stayed overnight in a motel in Syracuse. The next morning they were on the road again, crossing into Massachusetts and driving toward Cape Cod. A.D. thought Massachusetts was a beautiful state. She especially liked the wispy blowing scrub pines on Cape Cod.

"They smell so good," she told Mrs. Cramer.

They arrived an hour early for the ferryboat at Woods Hole. Mrs. Cramer got the car in line for boarding, then they walked around the wharves until the boat was ready to load.

Again, A.D. was impressed with smells—this time, the smells of the sea, delightful, breezy, fishy smells. She loved the sight of the docks, the water, the big white ships, the carefree smiling travelers walking the piers and leaning their luggage against the pilings, and dogs, dogs everywhere. Harold Poopsie would not be the only canine traveler on the ferryboat. She watched the white-and-gray sea gulls swoop to the dock, then fly up again into the sky, pause, glide onto a ship's rail. The noise of their wings sounded like small train engines. She looked along the Cape Cod coast at Woods Hole with its brilliant flowers highlighting the green grass cover, its small Cape Cod cottages, and some very large Cape Cod mansions.

"Why do we want to leave here?" she asked Mrs. Cramer.

"Because, if you can believe it, Nantucket is even nicer, better, prettier," Mrs. Cramer said.

A.D. shook her head. "I can't believe it." She laughed.

When the announcement for their boat came, they got into the station wagon to await their turn for loading. Soon they were driving into the belly of the ferryboat. After they were parked, they climbed up to the top deck. Mrs. Cramer held Stephanie by a child's halter, and A.D. held Harold Poopsie on his leash. They sat on green deck chairs, feeling the warm sun, eager for the boat's whistle that would signal their departure.

HOOOOT TOOOOT. Their boat ride began.

"I'm glad it's a nice day," Mrs. Cramer said. "I wanted you to meet Nantucket in its finest shining glory. We do get a lot of rain, you know."

"I know. Daddy told me."

"I like the rain on Nantucket as much as the sun. It's a good gloomy, pouring, pounding rain. I like to walk in it. I like to get soaked in it."

"Mother doesn't like me to go out when it's raining."

"We'll ride bicycles in the rain this summer."

They traded charges, and A.D. walked Stephanie around the top deck. Stephanie was eager to catch the sea gulls flying with the ship, so A.D. held tightly to her halter reins. She decided she loved the gliding feel of a moving ship.

They stopped to watch a young red-haired boy feed the gulls. He seemed to have brought a bag of bread especially for the birds. A.D. wished she had brought some bread. It looked like fun.

The boy saw her watching him and held out his bag to her. "Want to feed them?" he asked. She gratefully took a slice and she and Stephanie threw some to the gulls. The boy, quite experienced, had the gulls coming to his hand for the food.

A.D. picked Stephanie up and hugged her. "Isn't this great! Isn't it fun?" she cried.

They walked down and explored the second deck. There were staterooms here and maroon-padded benches filled with sleeping travelers, rest rooms, a snack bar, a water fountain.

They visited the snack bar several times in the next hour.

After they had passed Martha's Vineyard and were not yet in sight of Nantucket, A.D. stood up so she could fully appreciate the feeling of a sea voyage: no land in sight, a small yacht passing by now and then, still the following sea gulls flapping and soaring after the boat.

She breathed deeply, thinking life could not be more perfect. Stephanie had fallen asleep in Mrs. Cramer's arms, and Mrs. Cramer looked as if she might be nearing sleep herself. Her head rested on one of the wooden boxes that carried the life preservers. Her eyes were closed, and her face leaned into the sun.

Harold Poopsie's leash was hooked over A.D.'s wrist like a bracelet as she was drinking from a Coke bottle. She was savoring the soda, savoring the moment, when suddenly Harold Poopsie leaped away from her. Her wrist followed. The Coke bottle fell, Harold Poopsie barked, and A.D. screamed in surprise. A big woolly sheep dog appeared from under her chair. He seemed to have the idea in his head to eat Harold Poopsie. Harold Poopsie ran, A.D. ran, and the big white sheep dog chased them both.

Down the steps to the second deck they all ran. Soon there were four in the run. A tall boy ran after the sheep dog shouting, "Field! Stop, boy! Field!"

Harold Poopsie ran out onto the second-level deck and pulled A.D. after him. The leash tangled in a deck chair in which a man was sleeping. A.D. bent over him to extricate the leash, and when she got up the man's hairpiece was hooked on the button of her sweater. He woke up and put a hand on his now very bald head.

"My hair!" he exclaimed.

He got up and joined the chase. "Stop already!" he called. "My hairpiece. You've got my hairpiece."

His wife called after him, "You insisted on getting it wholesale."

Harold Poopsie ran past the snack bar, pulling A.D. The sheep dog followed. The tall boy followed the sheep dog. The bald man followed the boy. The dogs were barking. A.D. was yelling, "Harold Poopsie!" The boy was yelling, "Field!" The bald man was yelling, "My hair!"

Harold Poopsie turned the corner and led them down the steps to the part of the boat where the cars were parked. He ran between the cars, pulling A.D. after him. They finally stopped between a blue Chevy and a gray Olds because there was not enough room for A.D. to squeeze through. She was stuck, and all of Harold Poopsie's tugging at the leash could not budge her. The sheep dog ran into her. The tall boy caught the woolly dog. The man ran into the boy.

"My hair! Get my hair out of her sweater!"

For the first time, A.D. looked down and saw the weird hank of hair hanging there. She unhooked it from her button. She gave it back to the man. "I'm sorry," she said.

He adjusted it onto his bald head. "It's a very good hairpiece. I don't mind telling you I got it for two hundred dollars wholesale."

The tall boy spoke to A.D. "I don't know what got into my dog, chasing yours like that. Here, can I help you out? Are you stuck tight?"

A.D. backed out from between the Chevy and Olds. "Ah! I made it." She turned and looked up at the boy. She thought he was kind of cute.

"It makes me look ten years younger," the man said. "See?"

But A.D. was looking at the boy and the boy was looking at A.D.

"He's a nice dog," A.D. said, petting the face of the

woolly dog the boy was holding. "And he has a nice name. Field. I like it. It's a lot better than Harold Poopsie." She looked for Harold Poopsie. He was shivering under the blue Chevy.

"Don't feel bad," the boy said. "His real name is Horace Wonderdog, Champion of Fairlawn Field. Now you know why I call him Field."

A.D. laughed.

"What's your name?" the boy asked A.D.

"Adriana Prushtak. A.D. for short. What's yours?"

"Rod Zimmerman."

They smiled at each other in a happy, dazed sort of way.

The man had not left. He was holding his stomach. "Boy, do you notice how rocky the boat is down here? Is my face turning green? It feels green."

A.D. and Rod smiled and stared at each other. "Where are you from?" Rod asked.

The man rolled his eyes and ran to the side of the boat. He bent over the side. "Aau . . . gha . . . guh," he said.

As he leaned far out, delivering himself of his seasickness, his hairpiece delivered itself from his head. It fell as gracefully as a sea gull and, reaching a wave, floated lazily on the water.

"Hair overboard!" he yelled.

A.D. and Rod were softly laughing and talking. They didn't hear him.

The man shrugged his shoulders and patted his bare head. "It's going to be a lousy summer," he said as he went up the stairs.

Chapter Seven

Mrs. Cramer ran through the house like a child finding surprises. A.D. could hear her exclaim "oh" and "ah" and clap her hands in happiness.

"It's perfect!" she cried. "Just as I remembered it."

A.D. and Stephanie still stood in the long front hallway, surrounded by the suitcases, but Harold Poopsie was inspecting the house with Mrs. Cramer.

A.D. finally took Stephanie's hand. "Well, what are we standing here for? Let's see the house."

There were four rooms downstairs leading off the main hallway. To the left was the parlor. A beautiful oriental rug gave the large room a cozy feeling. Two blue wing chairs flanked a red love seat, with a fireplace opposite. An antique highboy and desk completed the furnishings. To the right, at the front of the house, was a library. Or if it wasn't a library, it should be called one, A.D. thought, for it was filled with books —books in shelves on each wall, books on tables, and there were two armchairs and two chaise longues with reading lamps. And a fireplace here too, nice for rainy days. It had been raining when they arrived on Nantucket.

At the back of the first floor a kitchen led off to the right and a dining room to the left. From the dining room were French doors leading onto a screened porch. The screening was almost entirely covered with a growth of ivy.

They took the stairs and found three bedrooms and a bath on the second floor. The large room on the left was Mr. and Mrs. Cramer's. Of the other two rooms, one would be Stephanie's and one A.D.'s.

"You take the back room," Mrs. Cramer said to A.D. "I want you to have the lovely view of the sea. It's the room I used as a young girl. Stephanie is too small to appreciate it."

A.D. was thrilled. The room looked as if it had come right out of another century. It had a charming old tester bed with a white lace coverlet and a white lace canopy. Small oriental stepping rugs were scattered about the wide wooden plank floor. Ruffled white curtains hung at the window. The room was wallpapered with small pink and yellow flowers and accented with white woodwork. A small old chest would hold A.D.'s clothes. Above it was a plain mirror in a wooden frame to match the chest. There was a small bedside table with an oil lamp on it, and a straight wooden chair sat near the bottom of the bed.

She unpacked her bags and took Dorothy out of the tote bag and fluffed her dress.

"Look, Dorothy! Our room!"

She placed the doll on the pillow of the canopy bed. "Dorothy, I'm so happy."

Mrs. Cramer came into her room. "I'm sorry your introduction to Nantucket was in the rain. I had such high hopes when we left Woods Hole."

"That's okay," A.D. said. "It'll probably be nice tomorrow."

"No, I don't think so. The caretaker said it's a squall. I think we'll be in for it for three days at least. Feel like dinner? We'll eat downtown tonight. Tomorrow we'll get in supplies."

They walked down the stairs.

"Mrs. Cramer, I know now why you wanted to come back here. There's something about it. I like it too, even in the rain."

"The furnace smells peculiar," Mrs. Cramer said.

A.D. gathered Stephanie into her arms and waited on the porch, protected from the rain by its overhang. She heard Mrs. Cramer put Harold Poopsie in the kitchen. "Be good. We'll bring you some dinner." She saw Mrs. Cramer walk into the parlor and run her finger along the back of the love seat.

"Aunt Harriet. Uncle Milt," she whispered.

She tapped the top of the blue chairs.

"Catherine. Cynthia."

She walked to the fireplace and turned toward the love seat. "Aunt Harriet, I'm going down to the town. I won't be long," she said.

Then she went out the door. "Oh, Adriana!" she said, surprised. "I thought you were already in the car."

Chapter Eight

It rained for a week with no letup. They saw Nantucket by car, driving all around the island, all the way to 'Sconset, where the pictures of the cottages with roses on the roofs had been taken for the travel pamphlets. They went antiquing. They visited the whaling museum, where they learned that Nantucket had been a great whaling center for over a hundred years. The business of whaling had begun in the 1690's, and by the 1790's the whaling ships had had to be very large and go as far as the Pacific Ocean to find enough sperm whales.

"In our house," Mrs. Cramer said, "think how lonely the women were, looking out to sea, hoping for a glimpse of the ships coming home. As whales became scarce, the men had to travel halfway around the world. Sometimes they were away from home two and three years at a time."

"It must have been awful for the women," A.D. said.

"The women in my family were strong. I come from

a long line of whaling widows. They had to be strong."

Stephanie pulled at them so they would stop talking and look at an old whaleboat and the jaws of an enormous sperm whale.

Another day A.D. helped Mrs. Cramer get in painting supplies because she wanted to touch up the woodwork in the house when the weather cleared. They also went bicycling in the rain and came home soaked, took hot baths, and sat before the fireplace cooking a meal of hot dogs and marshmallows.

A.D. thought Nantucket was enchanting. She only wished she had caught a glimpse of Rod Zimmerman that week. She had liked him on the boat, and every day she thought about him and wondered what he was finding to do in the rain.

Mrs. Cramer became increasingly upset about the smells that she said were coming from the furnace. She set A.D. about the house to sniff for them.

"Here, try over here," she said, pulling A.D. toward the heater outlet in the library room.

"I don't smell anything special," A.D. said.

"It's rubbery. Yet it's not rubbery. It's electrical."

"I don't notice anything unusual."

"Sniff. Plastic? You have to really sniff if you're going to smell anything. Breathe deeply. Expand. I wish Jerry were coming this weekend. He's good at smells."

"I wish I could smell it, Mrs. Cramer. Honest, I just can't."

Mrs. Cramer bent to look out the windows. "Well, we'll bolt the basement door. I don't want Stephanie going down there by mistake. There are poisons down there. Of course the problem is the wash. We'll have to use the laundromat downtown. I like things clean."

"I don't mind going down to do the wash for you, Mrs. Cramer."

Mrs. Cramer stamped her foot. "No, I forbid it. No one will go down to the basement. When Jerry comes, he'll fix it. I wonder why he isn't coming this weekend. Jerry can fix anything." She looked at the books on the east wall and seemed to be reading the titles with her lips. She stopped reading and stared at the floor for several minutes.

"I'm making sense, aren't I?" She held her head and lay down in a chaise. "Perhaps I just need to rest." She closed her eyes. "You must tell me, Adriana, if I start talking funny. I don't want to let go. I'm here in Nantucket, and I want to hold on. Help me, Adriana."

"I could make you tea," A.D. said.

Mrs. Cramer smiled, her eyes still closed. "Yes, tea. They always bring me tea."

"Who?" A.D. asked.

"Aunt Harriet and Catherine. They always brought me tea. Catherine is her daughter. My cousin. She's a year older. After Aunt Harriet and Uncle Milt died, she didn't want the place. That's how I got it. She was frightened one summer, said it was haunted." Mrs. Cramer laughed. "What do you think of that, Adriana?"

A.D. smiled. "I don't believe in ghosts."

Mrs. Cramer nodded. "Neither do I. I think. At least I never saw any. Catherine was always seeing them."

"Daddy says ghosts are the product of a very active imagination."

"Catherine was outwardly shy. But I think your father's theory could be right for her. She read a lot and fantasized. Do you read, Adriana?"

A.D. shrugged. "I sort of have to. It's the only way I can get my parents' attention. If they see me with my nose in a book, they always stop whatever they're doing and ask me all about it, and pretty soon we're talking about other things, and it gives me a chance to talk to them about something they otherwise wouldn't have time to talk to me about for days. So whenever I feel like talking, I start reading a book."

Mrs. Cramer clapped her hands and giggled. "I love it! I can just see you! That's a marvelous story."

"Mrs. Cramer," A.D. said softly, "you don't want tea now, do you?"

"No. Now I don't. Thank you, Adriana, for cheering me up. That's very nice."

"It's going to stop raining tomorrow. Can I help you paint?"

Mrs. Cramer smiled. "Why, thank you for remembering about it. Yes, if you like. If it does stop raining, you can help me in the morning, but I do want you and Stephanie to get to the beach in the afternoon. You'll both love it."

"Won't you come to the beach with us? It would be fun."

"Someday perhaps. Thank you very much, Adriana."

Chapter Nine

The rain stopped falling during the night. Next morning the sun was out, drying up the wet island. Stephanie and A.D. went out to the yard after breakfast. The yard, which extended about twenty feet to the sidewalk, was damp.

"Don't go on the grass," A.D. cautioned the little girl.

"Bike," Stephanie said, trying to get up on A.D.'s bicycle.

"Later on today," A.D. told her, "after we help your mommy paint."

A young man with a beard and blue tattered clothes walked along the sidewalk. He was dripping wet, as if he had just taken a shower with all his clothes on. Even his beard was dripping. Suddenly he turned and walked toward Stephanie.

The little girl looked at the young man. "Daddy," she said.

"Your daddy doesn't look like a hippie, Stephie," A.D. whispered.

"Hippie, hippie," Stephanie said, trying out a new word.

A.D. watched him. He looked to be about twenty, she thought, except for his eyes. They were penetrating eyes, the color of light blue. The eyes make him look thirty, she thought.

"Hi," she said to him.

He stopped watching Stephanie and looked at her. She smiled; then he did too.

"Finally a little sun," she said.

He nodded slowly. Then he spoke, although it seemed as if his mouth moved for several seconds before the sounds came out.

"Is Mim home?"

"Who? Mrs. Cramer?" A.D. asked.

"Mim. I've come for Mim Sooner. It's Richard. Tell her Richard's come for her."

"Gee, you must have the wrong house. There's no Mim Sooner here. And I don't know the neighbors' names. We've only been here a week, and it's been raining the whole time. I haven't met anyone."

"Mim's expecting me."

"She must live farther up the street."

The young man looked again at the house.

"Try farther up the street. Perhaps you got the wrong house number."

"Thank you kindly, miss. When Mim returns, please tell her Richard called for her."

"Well, okay," A.D. said, "but you do understand she doesn't live here? Just Cramers and a Prushtak for the whole summer."

The young man looked again at the house, as if he were looking right through it, his blue eyes penetrating the clapboards, searching for the girl he called Mim. Then he walked over to Stephanie and shook hands with her.

"Good-bye, little one," he said, and left.

" 'Bye, Hippie," Stephanie called.

A.D. laughed at her, then scooped her up and carried her into the house. "Now we are going to put you in the parlor and surround you with toys so you'll be happy while your ma and I paint."

Mrs. Cramer was in the hallway with a can of white paint and a paintbrush. "Hi," she said. "Your brush is in the kitchen. Oh, bring the newspapers, too, just in case we drip."

A.D. left Stephanie in the parlor with her favorite toys. Then she got the papers and paintbrush.

"I'll start the woodwork in the upper hallway," Mrs. Cramer said. "Do you want to start the stair railings?"

"Okay," A.D. said. "I can keep an eye on Stephanie if she leaves the parlor."

They worked silently for a while, sharing the bucket of white paint.

"When you're ready to work down the stairs, we'll have to get you a separate bucket," Mrs. Cramer said.

"Has the house been empty for a while?" A.D. asked. "I mean in the summers. Has anyone stayed here?"

"It was rented out by a real-estate agency for the two summers since Aunt Harriet died. But no more. I want to come here every summer."

"There was a man around today asking for a girl. I

bet she rented here last summer. He probably hoped she was back again. I kept telling him it must be another house, but he seemed to know where he was."

Mrs. Cramer stopped painting. "As I recall, three college girls rented the house last summer."

"He must have dated one of them. He really was disappointed."

"Can you see Stephanie?" Mrs. Cramer asked.

"I can hear her playing with her toys."

"Good. We'll get a lot done."

They worked for over an hour. A.D. did not bother to check Stephanie because they could hear her playing. Every once in a while her laughter made them both smile.

"She loves those toys," A.D. said.

When they finished the hallway, they counted the paint spots on their arms and hands.

"I have more than you," A.D. said.

"Yes! And a big white spot on your nose."

"No wonder it was itchy. You have a white streak across your forehead and on your hair by your right ear."

"Oh, no!" Mrs. Cramer laughed. "We're both a mess. Thank goodness Stephanie was occupied and didn't get into the act."

They went to the kitchen and cleaned the paint off the brushes and themselves.

"Now let's show Stephanie where she must not touch today," Mrs. Cramer said.

When they reached the parlor, Stephanie was stamping her feet and crying. "Come back! Come back,

Hippie!" She looked at her mother. "He's gone," she said, disappointed.

"Why, darling, no one's here. No one's been here. Adriana and I were painting the hallway."

"Hippie gone," Stephanie said.

"Oh," A.D. said, "that fellow I told you about who was looking for the girl from last summer. He had a beard and was dressed kind of funny. Stephie called him Hippie."

"Hippie play with me. Now Hippie gone."

"No," A.D. said, "the hippie didn't play with you. He only stayed a minute."

"Hippie here. He play with teddy bear."

A.D. smiled at Mrs. Cramer. "Imaginary friend?"

Mrs. Cramer nodded. "No one could have come in the front door. We would have heard."

"I want Hippie come back," Stephanie said.

Mrs. Cramer looked at A.D. "I'll make some lunch. Then you two can go to the beach this afternoon."

Chapter Ten

They rode to the beach on A.D.'s bicycle. Stephanie, in her pink two-piece swimsuit, picked up all the seashells she could find. She piled them on A.D.'s striped beach towel.

"Shells for Mommie," she told A.D.

"Let's not take the whole beach back to Mommie," A.D. said as the seashell pile grew higher and higher. "Why don't you take your little pail and shovel and dig a hole to China?"

A.D. turned onto her back. She leaned back on her elbows and looked out at the sea. Her green bikini matched the green stripe in her green-and-blue-striped towel.

She watched the slow blue waves touch the beach. They washed over the shiny smooth pebbles and seeped into the sand. A big ferry steamer was on its way back to the mainland. Sea gulls followed it. She felt happy. The warm sun made her sleepy. She turned to see Stephanie busily digging to China. I love this place, she thought.

"Hey! You've cornered the market in seashells," a voice said.

A.D. sat up. It was Rod Zimmerman.

"Hi!" she said.

"So you didn't melt in all the rain. I was afraid I wouldn't find you again." He sat down beside her in the sand.

She smiled. "Do you want to go swimming?"

"Who me?" he said. "Heck, no. I took a bath once. That was enough water for me."

"You're kidding. Come on, let's go swimming." She got up and tried to pull him up. But instead, he pulled her down.

"Are you trying to drown me? I tell you I can't swim."

She laughed. "I still think you're kidding. Aren't you?"

"Hey, did that kid you baby-sit come to the beach with any clothes on?"

"Of course," A.D. said.

"Look at her now."

A.D. looked. Then she wanted to die. Stephanie had her pink bathing suit off and was burying it in the sand.

"Stephanie!" A.D. ran for her and grabbed the bathing suit. It was covered with wet sand. She picked up the little girl and rushed her to the water. She washed off Stephanie and the bathing suit; then she dressed her again.

"Now this time keep it on," she said.

Stephanie pulled at the suit. "Wet," she said.

"I don't care," A.D. said. "Don't you dare take it off again."

"Come on over here," Rod called to Stephanie. "I'm going to make you a sand castle." He took her bucket and shovel and made an elaborate fort in the sand. A.D. and Stephanie helped him decorate it with seashells and straws and paper cups.

"We will have the finest castle on the beach," Rod said.

Stephanie forgot all about her wet bathing suit, and soon it was dry.

A.D. asked Rod where he lived on the island.

"I'm down here with my Uncle Unky. He's an artist. He rented a house on the road to 'Sconset. It has plenty of room for him to work, and I help him by staying out of his way. There are canvases and paint everywhere. Don't I smell like turpentine? He's getting ready for a one-man show in the fall. I don't know when he sleeps —maybe now while I'm at the beach. It seems to me that he works all night. Uncle Unky says he doesn't."

"Is he famous?"

"Well, he's sold some big things and won a few prizes. He seems happy."

"I didn't quite catch his name," A.D. said.

"Well, I call him Uncle Unky. His real name is Dan Daniels. But his artist name is Danny Dannielle. He likes a French sound."

"How'd you get Uncle Unky out of that?" A.D. asked with a laugh.

"What else? I couldn't say Uncle when I was little. I called him Unky. He used to scare me half to death. He's a big guy. He'd stare at me and scream, 'Kid, if you must call me Unky, you better put Uncle before it.' So it's a family thing. We all call him Uncle Unky now."

A.D. smiled. "What does he paint?"

"He's good with people and moods. He's doing a lot of boat things now, some of the old Nantucket houses, that sort of thing."

"I'd love to see his paintings. Does he ever let you watch him work?"

"I never thought about it. I think all artists are crazy, but I could ask. I don't know what he'd say."

Later, A.D. and Stephanie went swimming in the waves. Rod watched them from the beach.

"Come on in. It's fun," A.D. called, but he wouldn't.

When it was five o'clock, A.D. said they had to go home. Rod rode with them on his red bicycle.

"Now that I know where you live," he said," maybe I should pick you up for the beach tomorrow."

A.D. smiled. "Okay." She liked the way his dark hair fell across his forehead, practically covering his eyes. He was tall and thin, and he looked like a bunch of uncoordinated long bones riding his bicycle. Mr. Bones, she thought, and laughed.

"Well, Stephie, I'm going to give you a shower, and then I want you to take a nap before dinner," A.D. said. "Wasn't it fun at the beach?"

Stephanie started to cry. "Seashells," she said.

"Oh, no!" A.D. said. "We forgot them. Now don't worry. We'll remember to bring them home tomorrow. Don't cry. We'll find even prettier ones tomorrow."

The house was quiet, and Mrs. Cramer's bedroom

door was closed. A.D. figured she was resting. She quietly bathed Stephanie, then put her in bed for a nap.

A.D. sighed. She was tired. She decided to shower and rest a bit herself.

When she opened the door to her bedroom, she caught her breath and stood still. Her room was a mess. The clothes were half out of her drawers. The chair was turned on end. The bed canopy was pulled off and trailing to the floor. And the wallpaper, the lovely small-flowered pink-and-yellow wallpaper was in shreds, as if someone had scratched at it and torn at it and shredded it for all it was worth. So much was pulled off that parts of the wall were bare.

She closed the door and ran to the bed. She grabbed up Dorothy and hugged her. She stared at the room.

"Oh, Dorothy, you know what went on in this room today, don't you? You know, don't you? But you won't tell."

Chapter Eleven

Mrs. Cramer had good days and bad days. On the good days, she was so good that A.D. forgot there had been bad days. But the bad days were really bad, like the day she pulled the wallpaper off the wall in A.D.'s room. She hadn't remembered doing it, but her fingertips had bled for a week. A paperhanger was called in to repaper the room in a soft pink-and-white pattern.

A.D. did most of the work in the house now besides the work of caring for Stephanie. She did the laundry. She food-shopped. She cleaned the house. And she cooked. She didn't take any days off. She could have. She had a day a week coming to her. But she was afraid that Mrs. Cramer would not be able to cope with Stephanie. Coping seemed to be her problem. The only way A.D. knew to help her was to take most of the responsibilities from her and to take them on herself.

Mr. Cramer, who was supposed to have come every weekend, came only rarely. At those times, Mrs.

Cramer seemed to gather her strength so she could appear relaxed and normal for his visit.

A.D. wanted to tell Mr. Cramer that things were not quite right, but she didn't know how. He wasn't exactly approachable. He had a high forehead and a receding hairline. To A.D. his eyebrows seemed to line up with his sideburns, and there was a bushy moustache on his top lip. He went around the cottage smoking a pipe and frowning a lot. He always brought with him an attaché case stuffed with papers, and he spent all his time reading those papers and muttering either "I'll have to talk to Herm about this," or "I better call Harve about this."

A.D. finally learned that Herm was the president of Mr. Cramer's company and Harve was a vice-president who worked for Mr. Cramer. So Mr. Cramer was somewhere between a vice-president and a president. She thought perhaps his title might be Head of the Firing Squad, because whenever Mrs. Cramer asked something like "How are Jake and Lisa?" he would say, "I had to fire Jake last week." Or if she asked, "Is your new secretary working out?" he'd say, "I let her go yesterday."

Mrs. Cramer never said anything, but she often got a funny look on her face. A.D. could tell she was fidgeting inside and just about to lose her cool. But somehow Mrs. Cramer controlled herself, and things always seemed fine during Mr. Cramer's weekend.

But after Mr. Cramer left, Mrs. Cramer would settle into a deep depression. Sometimes she stayed in bed for days, just lying there and crying. A.D. would try to cheer her up, and when Stephanie napped, she visited with Mrs. Cramer in her room.

"The beach was filled today," she would say. Then she would tell Mrs. Cramer all about their day at the beach. She told her how many times they went swimming and how many walks they took and how many seashells they found. Mrs. Cramer listened intently to all of it. She seemed glad to hear about the beach, and she had met Rod several times and thought he was a nice boy.

"Maybe he'd like to come by some evening," she'd say. "You work so hard."

"I don't mind," A.D. would answer. "I think he goes downtown in the evenings."

"You should go downtown. I can hear Stephanie if she wakens."

"I don't mind. I like reading in the library room or the parlor. You have a lot of good books."

"I feel so guilty about you Adriana. You're so good to me. The least I could do is get better so you can go downtown with Rod some evening."

One day Mrs. Cramer told A.D. about her son who had died when he was five years old.

"We knew he wasn't strong, although he looked well enough. But he had a defect in his heart. We always knew he wouldn't live to be an adult, but though we knew he'd die, we never knew exactly when. He was five. I was having a bridge party that afternoon. It seemed that every room I cleaned he managed to spill something in, or somehow mess it up. I had invited a lot of women that I didn't know too well, and I wanted everything to be perfect. I wanted it to be more than perfect. Chris had been doing things wrong all morning. I got upset, and finally I screamed at him, 'You make me sick!' He gave a—a kind of cry. Like from here, his throat. He stretched out his arms. His lips moved as if he was trying to say Mommy. And then he fell down. He was dead. I said, 'You make me sick,' and he died.

"He was born in Philadelphia, and he died in Phoenix. Every time I hear that song about how long it takes to get to Phoenix I want to scream out, 'Five lousy little years!' I know you think I'm here in Nantucket because you can see me, but part of me is always in Phoenix with my Christopher Sooner."

"Is that what you called him?" A.D. asked.

"Christopher Sooner Cramer. His middle name is an old family name on my side. My maiden name was Cynthia Sooner Sanger. Stephanie's middle name is Sooner too. She was born twelve years after Chris died. I suppose I'm too old to be her mother."

"No, you're not!" A.D. insisted. "Honestly, Mrs. Cramer you look like twenty-five. You must be as old as my mother, but I can't believe it."

"I'm a year older than Ann," Mrs. Cramer said. "Chris would be nineteen if he had lived."

"I'm so sorry," A.D. said.

Mrs. Cramer smiled. "What's at the movies tonight? Maybe the three of us can go down after dinner."

"Oh, that would be great."

Mrs. Cramer got out of bed. "Yes. I'm going to get dressed. I feel better. Let's go to the movies."

64

So as the Nantucket summer moved from June to July, Mrs. Cramer had some good days and some bad days. Some bad days surprisingly turned into good days, just as sometimes the good days disappointingly turned into bad. A.D. took on more and more of the responsibilities of running the household. And she took on the greatest responsibility of them all, the job of trying to make Mrs. Cramer better.

Chapter Twelve

One morning in the second week of July, A.D. got out of bed, put on her robe, and went down to fix breakfast as usual. She set the table for Stephanie and herself and prepared a pretty tray for Mrs. Cramer. Then she stepped out the back door to pick a yellow rose. She found a small bud and placed it in a juice glass with some water. The tray looked inviting with its yellow place mat, the rosebud, and a sweet roll and half a grapefruit. She enjoyed making up the tray, especially since it seemed to please Mrs. Cramer. A.D. often tried to do things that would bring a smile to that lovely, troubled face.

She took the tray upstairs and lightly tapped on the door. There was no answer. She opened the door a crack. Mrs. Cramer was still asleep. A.D. placed the tray on the dresser, then went to look in on Stephanie just as she was climbing out of her crib.

"Morning, Stephie!" she whispered.

"Hi!"

"Hi, honey. Be real quiet. Your mommy's still asleep. Let's tiptoe down the stairs."

Stephanie liked to tiptoe. She quietly giggled all the way. She talked the whole time she ate her cereal. Then she drank her orange juice.

"More juice," she said when she had finished the glass.

A.D. got up to get the pitcher.

"A.D. cut," Stephanie said. "A.D. hurt. Stephie get Band-Aid. Poor A.D."

Adriana laughed. "You silly. I'm not cut."

"A.D. blood. Stephie put Band-Aid. Make better."

"Where? I'm not cut."

Stephanie got down from the chair. She pointed to the back of A.D.'s bathrobe.

A.D. twisted it around.

"Oh," she said. "I must have sat in something. Ketchup." But she knew she must have a funny look on her face. "Drink this new glass of juice, Stephie," she said. "I'll be back in a minute."

A.D. went upstairs. She took off the bathrobe and looked at the spot. In the mirror she saw another spot on the bottom of her pajamas.

"Oh, my gosh, I've got it," she said to herself. She took off her pajamas and put on her underwear. "Wait till I tell Linda. She got it at eleven. I thought I'd never get it. Oh, my gosh."

When she was dressed, she stood in the middle of the room, hugging her elbows, not knowing what to do.

She went out in the hall and called down to Stephanie. "Are you okay, Stephie?"

The little girl answered that she was playing in the parlor.

A.D. went to Mrs. Cramer's room and lightly knocked on it. There was still no answer. She tiptoed into the room and stood at the bottom of Mrs. Cramer's bed.

"Mrs. Cramer," she whispered. "Something's happened. Can you help me?" She felt almost like crying. "Mrs. Cramer? It's A.D. I need you."

Mrs. Cramer jumped to a sitting position. She looked wild-eyed and frantic. "What is it? What's wrong?" she demanded.

"Mrs. Cramer. There's blood. From there. It must be my periods. I don't have any pads, or whatever you call them."

Mrs. Cramer stared at A.D. Then she ran her finger through her messed hair. She looked confused. She blinked. Then suddenly she smiled, a big, warm, wonderful smile. She held out her arms, and A.D. stepped into them.

"It's all right. Dear Adriana. This is the first time it happened? Well, it should be a happy day. You have begun to menstruate. Now don't be alarmed," Mrs. Cramer said in an alarming way. "It's all perfectly natural, normal, and wonderful. I will take care of everything."

She jumped out of bed and put on her robe. Then just as fast she took it off. "What am I doing?" she muttered, more to herself than to A.D. "I have to go down to the drugstore. Adriana, you go to Stephanie. I'll be dressed in a second, and then we'll talk. And don't let a worry enter your head. This is a wonderful day."

A.D. walked down the stairs as though she were floating in a dream. It's happened to me, she thought, that thing that happens to all women. It's happened.

Mrs. Cramer was dressed in seconds. She ran down the stairs. She looked in at A.D. and smiled.

"How are you doing, honey?" she asked.

"Okay, I guess."

"I won't be ten minutes," she said as she breezed out the door.

When Mrs. Cramer returned, she showed A.D. how to attach the pad to her pants.

"Honey, it's going to feel strange for a while. But you'll get used to it. Give me your underwear and pajamas. I'll soak them in cold water."

A.D. went into the bathroom.

When she came out Mrs. Cramer said, "Well, do you feel grown up now?"

"No, just weird."

Mrs. Cramer laughed. "Now here's a calendar. We'll mark today. Then we'll count twenty-eight days and mark that."

"Oh, that's right. Twenty-eight days doesn't seem very long."

"The first year is unpredictable. Maybe it will be three months before it happens again. You'll have to be prepared. It can be fantastically irregular."

"Oh, no."

"Come on downstairs," Mrs. Cramer said, "I remember seeing an article in an old magazine. It would be good for you. It explains the whole thing. Let's see if we have it."

They went down to the library room, but couldn't find the magazine.

"That's okay," A.D. said. "I think I know enough about it."

But Mrs. Cramer insisted they all get in the car and drive down to the town library, the Atheneum.

They walked up the steps of the white-pillared, Greek-style building and asked for the magazine at the desk.

A.D. felt the pad slipping around, and she wanted to die. She was sure the librarian *knew*. She was sure everyone in Nantucket *knew*.

The librarian told them that they had passed the reading room. Mrs. Cramer went back and found the magazine.

When A.D. started to read the article she had to laugh. "My mom wrote this! She calls it 'As You Are About to Enter a Beautiful New World.' "

Mrs. Cramer smiled. "I know. I read it several months ago when it came out, and I thought that sounds just like Ann talking to Adriana. On a special day like this, I think your mother should tell you all about your growing up. Luckily we found the article."

"My mother won't believe I'm reading one of her articles. I never do."

"I'm going to take Stephanie downstairs to see the picture books. You get comfortable and enjoy your mother's words."

A.D. snuggled into the Windsor chair and began to

read. At first she felt embarrassed, but she smiled when she came to the part telling the circumstances of her mother's and grandmother's first menstruation. It happens to every woman, she thought, even my grandmother, even my great-grandmother and my great-great. It will happen to little Stephie someday. It is a special day, if somewhat weird. I like it and I don't like it. But I like what Mother calls it, entering a beautiful new world. I guess mostly I feel good about it. At least I'll never forget the way it happened and what everyone said and coming down here to the library and every crazy bit of it. Part of me is glad the *thing* has happened to *me*. *Finally!* But the other part—still sort of wishes it hadn't.

Chapter Thirteen

The next day A.D. got a letter from home.

Hi, Honey,

We had some excitement last week. My third book came out. It's the handbook for girls I told you about called *Things You Should Know Before You Are Twenty*. Brian thought it was a humor book. He's been reading it and giggling all day. Yes, he's in the house with nothing to do since he sprained his ankle when he and Kermit were playing chess. It's worse than when he had his tonsils out. At least then he wasn't yakking the whole time I was trying to write.

Dad misses his girl. He's going to wait to take his vacation till you get home so we can all go somewhere. Petoskey, I guess. How's that sound? Send us your vote. Brian wants to go to Frankenmuth. For two weeks? That's a lot of chicken. I know you'll want Cedar Point for one day. Okay. That's settled, but think what you want besides that. Gee, honey, we do miss you, but we guess you are having fun. Take some pictures, will you, so I can write a travel article about it.

You haven't caught cold, have you? Tell Cynthia no more of that bicycling in the rain. Linda's mother is having another baby. That makes ten???

I have to, ugh! clean today because I'm hostessing the Detroit Women Writer's summer workshop tomorrow. Wish you were here to HELP! The dust is swirling around my ankles. I'm really going to have a crowd. Already Elsie, Vera, Joan, Marj, Bettie, Iris, Marilyn, Naomi, and Doris have called. I'd better borrow some chairs. I'd also better muzzle Brian.

Let's see, have I told you all the news? Have I said I love you? Yes! I do! Have a marvelous time. It was 103 degrees here yesterday.

Love,

Mommie

A.D. decided to write right back.

Dear Family—

Well! So much has been happening since my last letter. Mother—private—I have entered your beautiful new world. Yes!! Don't worry. Mrs. C. was a real help. And I'm fine. Maybe I'll even develop a little shape on this lovely body.

Please don't tell me. Please just keep me in suspense. Only Brian could sprain an ankle playing chess. They were playing on the roof? Right?

Boy, Mother, does Mr. Cramer know Mrs. C. has problems? She's had some real bleary days, crying all the time, never getting out of bed. It's really serious, I think. Then all of a sudden, like yesterday, she'll snap out of it and be a doll. Sometimes

I just don't know what will happen. Listen, don't laugh, I'm not imagining all this. And don't write an article called 'Your Teen Can Too Help the Mentally Ill.' I'm really worried about her. Could you talk to Mr. C.? He's only been up two weekends, and when he's here, she's fine. Please tell me what to do!

Our routine's about the same. Unless it rains, I take Stephie to the beach. She's really a pretty good little kid. I think she likes me too. She tried to eat a bumblebee last week. (And then she sprained her ankle. Ha-ha, Brian.)

Remember I told you about Rod, the boy on the boat? He lives in Boston. Maybe Daddy can get transferred to Boston. Ha-ha, only kidding.

Gee, can't we get out of Mich. for vacation? It's fun to travel. Let's go west! Lake Tahoe? Chicago? Ann Arbor? Plymouth? West Livonia???

Hope your D.W.W. was fun. I think the ladies are super.

Special to Dad:

> *Nantucket Report*
> Breezes, balmy.
> Sea, calmy.

Dear people, I miss you. I love you. I'll be home in a month. Don't forget about talking to Mr. C. Really!

Love and kisses,
A.D.

P.S. Congratulations on your new book. I'll read it when I'm twenty-one, okay??? xxxxxxxxooooooooo kiss, hug, love, peace, me.

P.P.S. Did I tell you Mrs. C. was right about the furnace smell after all? When Mr. C. came, he smelled it too, and they called the heating co., and they smelled it too and replaced the thing that was stinking. Something about to blow out or up. Anyhow, everyone has decided my nose is completely inaccurate.

P.P.P.S. We still aren't allowed in the cellar. ??????

Chapter Fourteen

Every once in a while throughout the summer, A.D. would catch a glimpse of the bearded young man called Richard who had come to the house asking to see Mim Sooner. But she was never close enough to him to say hello, and when she tried, he seemed to disappear around a corner or into a shop. She actually wanted to speak with him again so she could tell him of the coincidence—that Mrs. Cramer and Stephanie both having Sooner in their names too.

One day while she was clearing up the breakfast dishes, she saw something out of the corner of her eye. Someone was in the backyard. She went to the window. It was the bearded Richard.

He wore the same blue clothes he had worn the first time she saw him. His head was bent toward a place on the ground halfway between the tree and the lilac bushes. He was digging with a spade.

A.D. watched him. Why is he digging? she thought. What is he doing in Mrs. Cramer's backyard?

She tapped on the window to get his attention, but he didn't seem to hear. She tried to open the window to call to him, but it was stuck. Most of the windows in the old house were stuck tight due to warping and their many coats of paint.

A.D. ran to the back door. She had to open it with the ends of her blouse because her hands were wet and could not move the knob.

When she reached the back steps, Richard was gone. She ran around the side of the house calling his name, but she did not find him.

She walked back to the place where she had seen him digging. The spade was lying where he had dropped it. He had not turned up much dirt.

I wonder what he was digging for, she thought.

She wasn't sure what to do. She was curious enough to want to keep on digging, but a strange cold feeling kept her from it. Instead she replaced the dirt and stamped it down. She carefully measured with her eye its exact position between the tree and the lilacs. Then she leaned the shovel against the back of the house and went inside to finish the dishes.

That afternoon at the beach Rod said to A.D., "Kid, you're disappearing right before my eyes. What are you trying to do? Get down to skin and bones like me?"

"Do you think I've lost weight?"

"Pretty soon you'll fit into Stephanie's bikini."

A.D. sighed. "I try to eat, but sometimes I just don't feel like it."

"You work too hard," he said. "You have to do too much. It's a rotten deal."

77

"Oh, no, honest, Rod," she said. "I want to do it. It's all my idea. Mrs. Cramer's never asked me to wash a dish or mop a floor or anything."

"She's never done it herself either."

"She did at first, but—oh, what's the use in talking about it. She's not well. Someone has to do it."

"If it was up to me, she'd be in the booby hatch where she belongs," Rod said.

"Oh, Rod."

A.D. got up and walked down to the water. A wave lapped over her feet. Rod joined her.

"Hey, Rod, your feet will get wet," she teased.

"Hey, yourself," he said, looking down at her in a protective way. "Would you and Stephanie want to meet me downtown tonight? Sort of a date to eat an ice-cream sundae?"

A.D. smiled. "Stephanie too? Rod, that's sweet. You know I wouldn't leave her. Well, we certainly do accept! What time and where?"

"Let's see. I have to do some errands for Uncle Unky, so how about seven thirty by the big anchor on the dock? I'll bring Field unless you want to bring Harold Poopsie."

"You bring Field. H.P. is too much trouble when I have to watch Stephanie. Hey, I bet this is Stephie's first date!"

Rod looked serious. "I know it's my first," he said.

"And mine," A.D. gulped.

They both became quiet and looked around self-consciously, trying to think of something else to say.

A.D., with Stephanie in her stroller, walked downtown early that night so they would have a chance to look at some of the shops. Stephanie liked the idea of shopping because A.D. promised she could pick out a toy.

"And I want to buy something for my mother and Dad and Brian," A.D. said, "so they'll have a souvenir from Nantucket. Stephie, do you realize our vacation will be over before we know it?"

"Toy!" Stephanie said. She clapped her hands together.

"I don't want it to end, Stephie. It's too wonderful here. Maybe we can drag each day out so that the time will go by more slowly."

"Toy toy toy toy toy," Stephanie sang in a sing-song voice. "Toy toy toy."

A.D. bought a dozen jars of rose-hip jelly for her mother, a small polar bear carved from ivory for her father, and a scrimshaw set and whale tooth for Brian. Stephanie picked out a magnet toy with black metal shavings inside a transparent case. The shavings could be moved around the man's face inside to give him a beard or sideburns.

They walked down to the wharf to meet Rod.

"Bandstand. Stephie go bandstand."

"Okay. Just once around," A.D. said. "Then we'll go up by the anchor. We don't want to be late for our date."

Stephanie climbed out of the stroller and ran around the bandstand. Then she ran to A.D., and they walked over to the anchor that stood in the stones by the wharf. A.D. sat on the wharf, and Stephanie climbed on the anchor.

The docked boats bobbed in the water. People walked up and down the boards. A.D. studied the weathered, wrinkled faces of the people in the boats. Sea people, she called them to herself. They're so beautiful and tough looking, she thought.

She breathed deeply of the sea air and looked at her watch. Rod was five minutes late.

Stephanie giggled and ran in a circle around the anchor. "Hippie!" she said, clapping her hands and giggling.

"Do you see that Richard?" A.D. asked, looking up eagerly at the people walking by. But only an older couple and two young boys carrying fishing equipment walked past. She stood and looked down the street. She could see neither Rod nor Richard. She looked at her watch again. "Gee, Rod's late," she said.

By eight o'clock she began to wonder if she had misunderstood where she was to meet Rod. She picked Stephanie up and placed her in the stroller. "Listen, we'll walk over to the clam place and around the dock, then back here. I can't understand why Rod isn't here. Something must have happened. He wouldn't just change his mind."

She pushed Stephanie up and down the docks until a quarter to nine. Stephanie fell asleep, and A.D. decided to go home.

As she passed the bandstand she was trying to decide whether to be mad or worried. Then she saw the white fluffy dog.

"Field!" she called.

He darted away and ran toward someone in the

shadows of the art gallery. The someone ran around behind the gallery, and as he did his face appeared for a moment in the light of the open doorway.

She saw that the running figure was Rod.

Chapter Fifteen

A.D. pushed the stroller back to the cottage. She lifted the sleeping Stephanie out and took her upstairs. She put on the child's pajamas without waking her and laid her in the crib.

Then she went to her own room, undressed, and put on her nightclothes. She lay down in bed and looked up at the canopy and began to cry silent tears. They moved around her cheeks and rolled down behind her neck and wet her pillow. She did not sleep until three o'clock.

The next morning she awoke late. Her eyes were red and swollen. She reached for Dorothy. She couldn't find her. She threw back the covers and hung over each side of the bed in turn looking for her.

"Dorothy!" she called. She got out of bed and crawled under it. Still no Dorothy. She felt through the covers again, being careful not to miss any lumps. She looked around the room. Half a cookie lay on the chair by the bottom of the bed.

"Stephanie," she said. "Stephanie must be up. She must have come in here and taken Dorothy!"

She jumped up, grabbed her robe, and threw it on as she ran down the stairs.

"Stephanie, where's Dorothy? You're a bad girl. Bring her here this instant!" She whirled around the the stair rail and ran into the kitchen.

There were dishes all over the kitchen table. A glass of milk was spilled, and there was a path of milk to the refrigerator. The big jar of peanut butter had been opened. Peanut butter was smeared on the tabletop and on the chairs.

"Oh, no," A.D. said. She rushed to the library room, then into the parlor. "Stephanie, answer me. Where are you? What have you done with Dorothy?"

She ran out the front door and around the side of the house. They were both on the back porch. Stephanie was singing Dorothy to sleep in her arms. Dorothy was covered with peanut butter and sopping wet with milk.

"Stephanie!" A.D. screamed.

"Shhh," Stephanie said. "My baby sleep."

A.D. yanked the doll away from Stephanie. "She's not *your* baby. Oh, look what you've done to her."

"My baby," Stephanie said. She stretched out her arms toward the doll.

A.D. stared at the little girl. "Dorothy belongs to me. She is private property. *Don't you ever touch her again.*"

A.D. went into the house and slammed the screen door. She took Dorothy to the kitchen sink and began to clean her up.

"Oh, Dorothy, this whole summer is turning out rotten. Rod last night and now look at you. I wish we had never come. I wish we were home."

She took off the doll's dress and began to wash it. She felt the doll's body. "Oh, it's soaked right through. Darn that Stephanie."

She put Dorothy under the faucet and washed her off. Then she took the dress and the doll upstairs. She opened her window, got a clean towel, and laid it on the windowsill. She put Dorothy on the towel.

"There's a nice breeze. You shouldn't take too long to dry out," she said. She went down to the kitchen to clean up the mess and to make breakfast.

After lunch, Stephanie said, "Beach, beach."

A.D. really didn't want to go to the beach. She didn't want to see Rod.

"I don't know, maybe not today," she said.

"Stephie want to swim. Beach."

"Well . . ."

"Goody, goody." Stephanie clapped her hands.

"Well. We can go to Children's Beach today. I don't want to go to the Jetties," A.D. said.

"Beach," Stephanie said happily.

When they were both in their swimsuits, A.D. told Stephanie to wait by the door. She went upstairs to check on her doll. Dorothy was still damp. She placed the doll in her tote bag.

"From now on, Dorothy, you're going with me everywhere. I don't want anything else to happen to you."

There were just a few children and mothers at Children's Beach. Stephanie waded at the edge of the water and collected stones in her sand bucket. A.D. leaned back on her elbows and watched the small yachts and sailboats bob on their moorings.

It's a lot nicer here, she thought, especially since Rod isn't here.

About three o'clock Stephanie lay down on her beach towel and went to sleep. A.D. covered her with her pink beach robe. She brushed a curl away from the little girl's forehead. She smiled. "Oh, Stephie. I don't blame you. I could sleep myself. It's nice here. But so boring."

A.D. sat up and drew pictures in the sand with her finger. She watched the sea gulls fly patterns against the sky. She took Dorothy out of the tote bag and dried her out in the sun. She heard the *toot-toot* of the ferry steamship and watched it leave for the mainland.

When Stephanie woke, they gathered up the towels and sand toys. Dorothy went back into the tote. They started for home.

"Well," A.D. said, "I guess Rod Zimmerman doesn't *own* the Jetties Beach. I guess we can go tomorrow if we want to. We certainly don't have to sit with him."

. Chapter Sixteen

The next day A.D. and Stephanie went to Jetties Beach. A.D. wore her rose-tinted sunglasses and avoided looking at anyone. She didn't want Rod to think she was looking for him. She didn't want him to think she was even aware he existed. Unfortunately, he was all she could think of.

A.D. placed the blue-and-green-striped beach towels on the sand. She sat on one and Stephanie ran down to the water. It touched her toes. She screamed with excitement and ran back to A.D.

"Swim!" Stephie said.

"Later. You play in the sand for a while."

"Okay," Stephie said. She picked up her yellow bucket and shovel. "A.D. make cakes," she begged.

They moved down to the wet sand near the water. A.D. packed the sand into the bucket, turned it over, removed the bucket, and a sand cake was baked. As fast as A.D. could make a sand cake, Stephanie sat on it. Make a cake. Sit on it. Make a cake. Sit on it. They were doing it so fast they both got to giggling and couldn't stop.

"Stephie do cake," the little girl begged.

"No!" A.D. said "I'm not going to sit on them!"

They got to giggling again. When they walked back to the beach towels, A.D. thought she saw Rod out of the corner of her eye. But she didn't get a good look.

"Seashells," Stephie said.

"Okay, but don't go too far."

In a few seconds Stephie was back. "Look, A.D., I found," she said.

A.D. looked up. Stephie was pulling Rod toward her.

"Come on, Rod," Stephie said. "Sit."

They looked at each other for a long moment, then Rod said, "I think I owe you a sundae."

"That's okay," A.D. said softly, shrugging her shoulders.

Rod sighed. "I don't know why I didn't come over to you. But when I saw that guy . . . I don't know. I just burned. I felt so stupid after. You have a right to talk to whomever you want. I guess I didn't like the looks of him. I'm sorry."

A.D. was puzzled. "I wasn't talking to anyone. Just Stephie," she said.

"That guy with you," Rod insisted.

"I'm confused. You think I was talking to someone at the anchor where I was supposed to meet you?"

Rod nodded.

"That's crazy! There were a lot of people walking by but nobody I knew. It's ridiculous."

"Look, I don't want to fight about it. You can talk to

anyone you like. But I saw him. Playing around the anchor with Stephanie and everything."

A.D. shivered and a chill went up her back. "Rod, I'm scared. What did he look like?"

"Come on," Rod said. "Forget it."

"No, I'm serious. I want to know what he looked like. I remember Stephie saying 'Hippie' and—oh, Rod! He looked like a hippie, didn't he? With a beard and funny blue clothes?"

"Yeah, he was a real ding-a-ling."

"Rod, I'm telling you the truth. *I didn't see him.* But I know who he is. I've even been looking for him."

"How could you miss him? He was right *there.*"

"Rod, something funny is going on, and I'm scared. Would you swear on the Bible that you saw him with us that night?"

"Yes."

"I would swear he *wasn't* there. Do you know what that means, Rod? Do you know what I'm thinking?"

"That one of us is a liar?"

"No! Look, let me begin at the beginning. Gee, when did it start? We had only been in Nantucket a week. I know—the day it stopped raining. That was the day I first saw him. It must have stopped raining in the middle of the night. But he was soaking wet. He was dripping. Stephie and I were sitting on the front steps. He came walking by and asked to see a girl. 'Mim Sooner,' he said. 'She's expecting me,' he said. I didn't know it then, but Sooner is an old family name of Mrs. Cramer's. Stephie's middle name is Sooner. I told him he was at the wrong house. He left, but I don't think he believed me. Rod, Mrs. Cramer had a son who died when he was five years old. Her son would be about the age of that hippie by now. Do you think he's come to haunt the Cramers?"

"A ghost? Oh, A.D. There's no such thing."

"Well," A.D. said.

"Besides, I never heard a ghost story where the dead person aged! I think he'd have to come back as a five-year-old ghost," Rod said. Then he laughed. "You're too much, A.D." he said.

"Well, maybe it's another ghost."

"What's with all this ghost stuff?"

A.D. stood up. "Let's walk up along the seashore," she said. She and Rod each held one of Stephanie's hands. They walked on the wet sand, the water washing their feet with each wave. Two small clouds were in the blue sky. The sun was hot on their arms.

"Of course I don't believe in ghosts," A.D. told Rod, "but Richard seems to appear and disappear so fast."

"Richard?" Rod said.

"He told me that was his name. The first morning. When he asked for Mim Sooner."

"Where else have you seen him?"

"Sometimes in the town. One day he was digging in the backyard."

"No kidding?" Rod asked.

"I know where if you want to try it," A.D. said.

Rod started to laugh. "This thing is really wild. You've got to be kidding."

"Aren't you curious? Why would he dig in Mrs. Cramer's backyard?"

"Because he buried Mim Sooner there!" Rod said, laughing.

A.D. had to laugh too. "I guess I am letting my imagination run away with me! I forgot to tell you, the house was rented out to three college girls last summer. Probably one of them was called Mim Sooner. I guess it's just a coincidence. I'm getting like Mrs. Cramer's cousin, Catherine. It was supposed to be her cottage, you know. She didn't want it. One summer she saw ghosts."

They both laughed. Rod picked Stephie up and held her in the air. "Whee," he said. "See Stephie fly like a birdie."

"Whee!" Stephie said.

A.D. looked at Rod. "But why didn't I see him? Oh, never mind," she said.

They turned around and walked back to the beach towels. A.D. and Stephanie went down to the water and jumped some waves. Rod built another sand castle for Stephanie. About four o'clock they decided to go home.

"I'll ride you up to the cottage," Rod said.

"Okay."

When they got to the Cramer cottage, Rod said, "I still owe you that sundae."

A.D. thought a bit, then she said, "Rod, come around back. I'll show you where Richard was digging. Are you game enough to see what he was digging for?"

Rod laughed. "I thought you'd forgotten about it."

"Come on," A.D. coaxed. "There's a spade in the yard. I was going to dig myself, but I was too scared."

Rod got off his red bike and dropped it to the ground.

"Okay, ghostie, here we come."

They walked to the backyard. Rod grabbed the

spade. A.D. stood between the tree and the lilac. "Here," she said.

He started to dig. Shovelfuls of dirt were piled onto the grass. When he had dug down about a foot, he said, "There's nothing here. You sure it's the right place?"

A.D. nodded. "Just try a little bit more."

He started digging again and hit something hard.

"A rock," he said. But when he dug it out, they saw it was a square tin box, like an old can for storing flour or cookies. Rod hit the lid several times with the spade till he was able to pry it off. Inside was a small wooden chest in the shape of a trunk.

A.D. brushed off the mold. "Oh, Rod. It looks like a miniature pirate chest."

Rod leaned the spade against the tree. "Well, I sure never thought we'd find anything."

The wooden chest was about eight inches long and four inches wide and six or seven inches high. The wood was dark, and when A.D. had finished brushing it, she could see brass nails in rows on its curved top.

"It must open with a key," Rod said.

"And we don't have a key." A.D. sighed.

"Is there a screwdriver in the house?" Rod asked.

"Oh, do you think we should pry it?"

"Well, we've gone this far. Don't you want to know what was buried here? How are you going to stand not knowing what's in the chest?"

"You're right! I'll see if we have a screwdriver." A.D. ran to the house.

"Bring a hammer too."

"Okay."

She had been gone just a second when she appeared at the screen door. "Rod, we can't," she said.

"Why not?"

"I don't know. I have a strange feeling that it's private or something. I can't explain it."

"Do you want me to bury it again?" he asked, a little exasperated.

"No. It's too pretty to cover. I'll keep it on the small dresser in my room. It would look perfect there. I wonder . . . if that's where it belongs?"

Rod shook his head and sighed. He replaced the dirt and set the spade and tin box against the house. He smiled uneasily at A.D.

"I told Uncle Unky I was in trouble with you. He says if you'll let me off the hook, he'll let you come and see his paintings. Next time it rains, he says."

"Oh, Rod! That's great! Can I bring Stephie? Can I bring Mrs. Cramer too? She loves art."

"Sure. But look, don't expect much. He's no Picasso." He looked down at his hands and made fists, pounding them together. His face turned pink. He took hold of A.D.'s arm. "Hey, are we made up now?" he asked.

She smiled and nodded.

He smiled too. "Well, I'll see you at the beach tomorrow, or if it rains, I'll come by and take you to Uncle Unky's."

" 'Bye!" A.D. called as he started around the house. "See you tomorrow."

Chapter Seventeen

A.D. thought it would never rain. Ever since Rod's Uncle Unky had said they could visit his studio on a rainy day, the days had been beautifully sunny. But rain is never too far from Nantucket, and five days after Rod extended the invitation, it poured.

Rod came on his bike to pick them up. A.D., Stephie, and Mrs. Cramer put on their yellow slickers, got on their bicycles, and followed Rod to his place.

"Is your uncle married?" Mrs. Cramer wanted to know.

"I'm glad you asked," Rod said. "Don't mention that word around him. He'll blow his top. He's separated and very bitter."

"I'm glad I asked," Mrs. Cramer said. "I don't want to get him angry. I think he's wonderful to let us all barge in to see his work."

"Well, he can get moody. But I think he'll be okay today," Rod said.

"Rod, everything will be fine. Don't be nervous," A.D. said.

"I'm not nervous." He paused. "No. You're right. I *am* nervous."

They all laughed.

"Well, here we are," Rod said. He jumped off and leaned his bike against the house. Mrs. Cramer and A.D. did the same. Then A.D. unbuckled Stephie's belt and lifted her down.

Rod took them into the house. He led the way to the back, where his uncle used two of the rooms as an art studio.

A big man who looked more like a prizefighter than an artist filled the doorway to the studio. One shoulder leaned against the woodwork. With the other arm he seemed to be holding up the top molding. He looked at the visitors with twinkling eyes.

"Hi!" he said. "I'm Uncle Unky. Call me Danny." His smile was wide and friendly. His hand let loose of the molding and came down to pat his big stomach. He burped loudly. "Come on in. Take a look at my work. Ask me any questions."

A.D. and Mrs. Cramer went into the studio. Stephie stayed with Rod in the living room. There were finished canvases hanging on the wall and stacked in the corners of the room. Some were set up on easels in the middle of the room. The pictures were startlingly realistic scenes of Nantucket. One whole wall held a series of sea-gull studies. They were flawless, brilliant. Mrs. Cramer was overwhelmed with their beauty. She took A.D. by the hand and discussed the pictures with her quietly, pointing out the fine quality of them, the exquisite strokings of the artist's hand.

"Hey, Rod!" his uncle bellowed. "Get everybody a beer."

Mrs. Cramer stared at him. "At ten o'clock in the morning?" she asked. "Besides, A.D. doesn't drink beer."

"*You'll* have one with me, won't you, Mrs. Cramer?" he urged.

Mrs. Cramer looked as if she wanted to say, "You're impossible. No wonder your wife left you," but instead she laughed and almost with a blush said she would try a morning beer.

This gesture made them friends. A.D. was left to look at the pictures in solitude. Rod's uncle conducted a personal tour of his paintings for Mrs. Cramer. They discussed his work, the work of other artists, Nantucket history, and many other things. They talked all morning. Rod and A.D. played with Stephie, and when the rain stopped, they took a short walk.

"I'm hungry," Stephie said.

"Let's head back and see what's in the refrigerator," Rod said. They went back to the house and had a snack.

Mrs. Cramer and Rod's uncle were still engrossed in art talk. "I can't get over how much that house," A.D. heard Mrs. Cramer say, pointing to one of the paintings, "looks like our house."

"I'd like to sketch *you*," Danny said.

Mrs. Cramer straightened in surprise.

"You say yours is an old family on the island," he continued. "You must have had an ancestor who looked like you. I'd like to sketch you, maybe put you on a captain's walk, looking out to sea, waiting for the return of your husband's whaling ship. Your face is significant. It says something."

"I'm sure my ancestors looked out to sea many times as they waited for the whaling ships to come home."

"You didn't say whether I can sketch you," Danny interrupted in a taunting voice. "What do you want? Compliments? Should I say you're beautiful?"

It became very quiet, and A.D. wondered what Mrs. Cramer was thinking. Rod was right. No wonder his uncle was separated from his wife. He didn't understand women. She heard Danny sigh and move around the room. He went to get a sketch pad and some charcoal.

Danny began to sketch and didn't seem to mind A.D.'s watching him. He sketched Mrs. Cramer in many different poses. As soon as he had filled a sheet of sketching paper he went on to the next one. Finally, after three hours, he had a picture that he would later do in oil. He showed the sketch to Mrs. Cramer.

She looked at it. She looked at Danny.

"You're very good," she said. "There's just one thing. The women in my family were strong. You have drawn a lonely, frightened woman."

Danny pulled up a box and sat down directly opposite her.

"I drew your face," he said, in what was a kindly tone for him.

"But you couldn't have," she insisted. "I was posing as I thought they would look. They were strong women, and I tried to project that strength in my face."

"Do you know what I think?" he asked gently. "I think those women, when they looked out to sea hoping to see the whaling ships, I think they were not strong. I think they were ordinary human beings who had been without their husbands for two, three years. I think they feared the worst, that the ship would never return. I think they were lonely and frightened. I think they looked the way you look. Lovely and lonely and frightened." He reached out and touched her face, his finger tracing the line of her cheekbone.

Mrs. Cramer stood up. "A.D., are you ready? We're going now."

They walked our to their bikes. A.D. told Rod, "We can find our way back. Thanks for today and thank your uncle."

As A.D. rounded the bend, she looked back and saw Rod still standing by the house. She waved. Then she pedaled up beside Mrs. Cramer.

"Isn't Mr. Danielle's work beautiful? I'd love to own one of his paintings. Didn't you just love them?"

Mrs. Cramer calmly pedaled her bicycle. "I think," she said, carefully choosing each word, "that he is a very talented artist."

When they reached the cottage, Mrs. Cramer went to bed and wouldn't eat any dinner.

Chapter Eighteen

One evening, when A.D. was reading in the library room downstairs, she finished a book that left her crying. She put it on the bookshelf reluctantly, wishing the story had not ended, wishing it would go on and that she could remain in its spell forever. She hugged her arms and walked around the room thinking about the book, feeling as if she were enclosed in a misty dream. She came to a stop in front of the shelves on one wall and ran a finger across the books. Her finger stopped on a thick, worn-leather book. The Holy Bible. She had never seen such a large Bible.

She lifted it down, almost falling backward with the weight of it. She dropped it on one of the chaise longues, then sat down and began turning the pages. She read a few of her favorite verses, but they didn't sound the same. She leafed through some more pages, and came to the middle of the book where there were sections for recording births, marriages, and deaths. The entries had been made in an elaborate old-fashioned script.

Each name was beautifully drawn like a carefully shaped art piece. Some of the names were interesting. Caroline Maud, Obadiah, Jesse, Israel, Prudence. Then she saw it: *Mim*. Mim Priscilla Sooner, born February 11, 1799.

A.D. felt as though her eyes were sewn to the words. She read them again, then over and over again. So there was a Mim Sooner. There really was a Mim Sooner. But she had lived a long time ago.

A.D. scanned the marriages. Nothing there about Mim. But she found her again in deaths. It simply said, "Dear Mim, January 20, 1834."

It could be assumed then that Mim had not married, A.D. thought. But she wondered if possibly she had once loved a boy named Richard.

There was nothing more in the Bible. Perhaps the answer lay in the old chest they had found in the backyard. It was on the dresser in A.D.'s room now. She closed the big Bible and put it back on the shelf. She went to her room and picked up the little wooden chest. She held it to her ear and shook it. There was a noise. Something was inside. And now A.D. wanted to know what it was.

What kind of key would fit the lock? she wondered. Where would such a key be now? Lost after all the years, or still here, somewhere in the house?

What would *I* have done with the key? A.D. thought, if I had buried the little chest in the backyard? Perhaps it was buried somewhere else in the yard in its own secret place. Or was there a secret place in the house? Like . . .

She sighed. "Oh, it could be anywhere. It could be

nowhere. Behind a book in the library room. Down in the forbidden cellar. It's hopeless."

She opened a drawer in the dresser and took out a bobby pin. She put it in the lock and wiggled it. One twist, and something clicked. When she pulled on the lid, it lifted.

A musky old smell reached her nose. The inside of the lid was crumbling. Small pieces of crisp, torn, umber-colored paper fell in her lap.

Her heart beat faster. It's old. It's very old, she thought. She pulled out a piece of material. It was a square with lace corners. A handkerchief. She studied the rolled edges.

"Someone made this by hand," she said.

Underneath the handkerchief was a smaller box. It was also wooden and seemed to be hand-carved. She carefully pried open its warped sides. A locket lay inside, a gold locket on a long gold chain. Her hands were shaking as she lifted it from the box. She wiped off some mold on her skirt. The locket felt smooth like a stone washed by the sea. It had an oval shape, and there was a small red stone in its middle. A garnet? She held the locket up to her neck and looked in the mirror. It was lovely. Plain, yet beautiful.

A.D. looked into the chest again and saw one more thing. A folded yellowed piece of paper. She touched it and its edges crumbled. Carefully she lifted it and opened it. Though it was faded and smudged, she could still read the handwritten message, "My father has made Richard unavailable. I shall die before he returns, of the worst sickness, love."

Quickly A.D. put the note, locket, and handkerchief

back in the chest. She closed its lid. She touched the brass nails and shivered.

She felt strangely like an intruder. She wanted desperately to talk with someone about these things, but she didn't want to bother Mrs. Cramer. She would have to wait until the next day, when she could tell Rod.

As soon as Rod came to pick her up for the beach, A.D. showed him the contents of the wooden chest.

"Rod, I think I have it figured out," she said. "See, this girl Mim is in love with Richard. Only her father doesn't approve of Richard, so he does something to prevent them from seeing each other, like a sort of shanghai onto a whaling ship. The father thinks Mim will forget Richard by the time he gets back home 'cause he could be gone a couple of years. But the thing is, he never gets home, because the ship sinks or he is somehow lost overboard, something like that. Mim never marries anyone else because Richard is her own true love. And Richard is a troubled ghost, coming back here to Nantucket year after year, confused and wanting to find Mim at this house. What do you think, Rod? It's logical, isn't it? I was awake half the night putting all the pieces in the puzzle together."

Rod just looked at her.

"Rod, that's got to be the way it happened," A.D. insisted.

"Oh, boy," said Rod, rubbing his forehead. "That joker must be having a good laugh now."

"What are you talking about?"

"This whole crazy mess is somebody's idea of a practical joke, that's what. That character dropping around asking for Mim Sooner, planting the name in your brain. Then showing you where to dig. So we dig. And we find more planted clues."

"But the name in the Bible," A.D. insisted. "That wasn't planted. Sooner is an old family name of Mrs. Cramer's."

"You're not the only one to read that Bible," Rod said. "This place has been rented out, you told me yourself. Somebody saw the Bible and thought what a huge joke to haunt you with a made-up ghost. He probably got the locket in a cheap antique shop. Yeah, and wrote the phony message too. 'I shall die from the worst sickness, love.' He must have had a really good laugh when he thought up that one."

"Rod, you're so stubborn," A.D. said.

"And you're so gullible," he said.

They sat down on the front-porch step. A.D. put the note and locket and handkerchief back in the wooden chest.

"There's one thing, Rod," A.D. said softly, "Why would someone I don't even know go out of his way to fool me?"

Rod poked at a weed that was growing through the step. "People get their kicks in strange ways."

"I don't know. I may not be exactly right in my theory, but I feel Richard is mysterious. I don't believe in ghosts, and yet I think that's what he is, a troubled ghost. You've heard about them, haven't you? They can't move on to the other world until they are at peace with this one."

"Look, A.D., I think Stephie is the only one who knows what she's talking about. She calls him Hippie, and I think that's all he is. Come on, let's go down and soak up some sun."

They went to the beach. But A.D. was not convinced that the Richard thing was a hippie's joke on her. She kept thinking about his penetrating eyes the first time she saw him and the way he expected Mim to be at the house waiting for him. He'd have to be an awfully good actor, she thought.

"Rod," she said finally, "maybe he is a hippie. I don't know. I do know I want to give him the box and what's in it. If it's all a joke on me, I don't care. Will you help me find him? Will you go with me?"

Rod smiled at her. "Sure. I know it's eating away at you. Sure, I'll go with you."

They decided to try looking for Richard that night.

Chapter Nineteen

After dinner A.D. put Stephanie in the stroller and waited in front of the Cramer cottage for Rod. He rode up on his bike and parked it by their front door.

"Ready?" he greeted them.

A.D. nodded and smiled. "Ready," she said. She patted her tote bag, which contained both Dorothy and the contents of the wooden chest. She had decided to keep the chest on the dresser upstairs, because it looked as if it belonged there. But the note, locket, and handkerchief she would give to the young man calling himself Richard, if they could find him.

Mrs. Cramer appeared at the front door. "Have a nice time downtown," she called.

A.D. and Rod smiled to her. Stephie waved. " 'Bye, Mommy. I love you." She blew a kiss to her mother.

The darkness was moving in earlier in the evenings now. They walked briskly down the hill and into the town to have as much daylight as possible for their search for Richard.

A.D. almost had a skip in her walk. "I feel like—I don't know what! Something! It's a very special evening, don't you think?" She reached down and tickled Stephie's neck. "Look for the hippie, Stephie. We want to find him. It's very important."

Rod had his hands in his pockets. "Just our luck, we'll find Casper the friendly ghost instead of Richard the hippie ghost."

A.D. looked sideways at him and teased, "See, Rod, you're a converted ghost believer already!"

They turned onto Lower Main to go toward the wharf. They didn't see Richard.

"Let's go up Main," Rod said. "I've seen some hippies hanging around farther up."

A.D. turned Stephie's stroller around, and they walked up Main Street. They looked at the people sitting on the benches outside the shops. Halfway up Main, Stephie pointed and said, "Hippie."

Rod and A.D. stopped and looked. Richard was across the street on the bench outside a restaurant.

"Oh, Rod," A.D. groaned, "he's with a whole group."

"I told you he hangs around with the weird ones. Let's forget it."

A.D. began pushing the stroller again. "Oh, I don't care. Let's go over and get it over with. Maybe he just sits with them so he won't be noticeable."

Rod shrugged his shoulders. "It's your party," he said.

They crossed the cobblestone street.

"Bump, bump, bump," Stephie said. "Hi, Hippie!"

The young man, Richard, turned and stared at

Stephanie. Then his face showed recognition. He got up and held out his arms to her. She jumped out of the stroller and put her arms around his legs. He bent down and patted her head. He looked at A.D.

"She is my little friend," he said.

"Richard," A.D. said, "I have something for you." She took the articles out of her tote bag and put them in his hands.

He did not speak, but stared at them, as if he were staring right through them.

"I want you to have them," she said. "I mean, you should have them. They are yours and Mim's."

Richard put the locket around his neck. A girl who had been sitting on the bench beside him examined it and called the others to look at it. "That's really *it*, Richard. You are it, Richard. Very it, baby," she said. They all laughed.

A.D. frowned and bit her lip. "Well, good-bye, Richard. I hope—I hope it's been fun for you." She turned the stroller around.

"Wait!" Richard said. "What about Mim? You saw her, didn't you? Did she have a message for me?" He looked as if he wanted to grab her and shake her, but he didn't touch her. Only his eyes pierced hers.

A.D. studied his face. What is real? she thought. Is he what I think, or is he one of them? The blue of his eyes almost hypnotized her. When her mouth opened, she didn't even know what she was going to say.

"Mim said not to worry. She said she loves you, Richard. She'll always love you."

A certain peace seemed to come into his face. He

smiled at A.D. "Then I can go," he said. He seemed so free, so relieved.

She nodded. "Yes. You are free to go."

He started walking in the direction of the wharf. He wore the locket. He held the handkerchief in his left hand and the note in his right. A.D. thought, He's going back to the sunken whaling ship. He'll walk into the water until it covers him, and we won't see him anymore. She suddenly covered her eyes, not wanting to see, not wanting to know.

"Rod," A.D. said, "I don't think we really have to know about Richard. Let's go home. I mean, if he's really a ghost, I don't want to know. And if he's just a hippie playing a joke on us, well, I don't want to know that either. Let's go home and not look back. I want to sleep nights."

They turned and walked the other way. They were silent for three blocks.

Then, "An unsolved mystery," Rod said, smiling.

"Yes," A.D. laughed. "Sometimes they're the best kind." She shivered in the warm evening.

At midnight a soft rain began to fall. The winds soon rose to gust level, the rain beat faster, and the weather did not clear up for four days.

Chapter Twenty

The Nantucket summer was almost over. Mr. Cramer flew up to Nantucket on a Tuesday. He would spend Wednesday, Thursday, and Friday vacationing, then start the homeward drive with all of them on Saturday.

It saddened A.D. to be going, and yet she missed her family. Seeing Mr. Cramer reminded her of them and of the letter she had written, and she wondered if her mother had said anything to him about Mrs. Cramer's condition. He didn't seem to look at A.D. at all. But she couldn't remember that he ever had.

Mrs. Cramer was up now that he was here. She was straightening up things and doing the cooking and beginning to pack and getting the house ready for closing. A.D. wanted to help, but Mrs. Cramer wouldn't let her. It was her job to do these things, she insisted, and she was going to do them.

A.D. had almost nothing to do now, except care for Stephie. It was so easy these last few days! She really felt that she was on vacation.

Friday morning Danny Dannielle knocked on the cottage door. He brought a painting for Mrs. Cramer. Mr. Cramer looked at him as if he had bad breath, but Mrs. Cramer was very excited.

The painting had been wrapped for the trip with thick padding.

"But I want to open it now," she said. "I can hardly wait till we get back to Pittsburgh to look at it."

"Livonia," Mr. Cramer corrected her.

"Can we open it, Mr. Dannielle?" she asked the painter. "Could you fix it all up again for me?"

Does she like Danny Dannielle or doesn't she? A.D. wondered. Or is she just putting it on because Mr. Cramer is here?

"You can't expect him to do that," Mr. Cramer said, taking charge.

"Why not?" Danny said, ripping it open. "Anything the little woman wants is my pleasure." He was teasing, but Mr. Cramer had the look on his face that he had when he was about to telephone Harve or Herm or someone.

Mrs. Cramer stared at the painting. It was the one he had sketched of her. But the face—the face was different from the one he had sketched. It was hers all right, but it was a strong face, a face full of strength and resolution and peace.

"You did it the way I asked," she whispered, impressed. "I thank you. I thank you with all my heart." She looked at Danny. She was happy, but her eyes were gentle and sad.

"I call it 'This Ship Will Not Sink,' " he said.

"I like that. 'This Ship Will Not Sink.' " She laughed

softly. "It will be my motto when I'm low. This ship will not sink! It gives me strength. You've given me something to hang on to, Mr. Dannielle. Thank you," Mrs. Cramer said.

Danny started to wrap it again for her.

"No," she said, "I want to see it. I'll put a blanket around it for traveling. But when we stop for gas or for the night, I want to be able to take off the blanket, and say, 'This ship will not sink!' "

A.D. noticed that after Danny had left, Mr. Cramer looked exasperated, but all he said before he went back to his attaché case was "How much have you seen of that creep this summer?"

Later that day Mrs. Cramer collapsed under the strain of packing and took to her bed. Mr. Cramer kept trying to coax her up, but she wouldn't move. He paced back and forth from the parlor to the library, and finally he turned on A.D.

"You haven't done enough to help Cynthia this summer. Maybe that's why you had time to write all those letters to your mother, going on and on about Cynthia's condition. I've noticed you since I've been here. Cynthia's been doing all the cleaning and dishwashing and packing. You go off swimming at the beach. Well, I hope you've had a nice easy summer. Do you really think you've earned the salary Cynthia's been paying you?"

He stopped for breath. But A.D. couldn't say anything. Her eyes burned. Her throat tightened. Her stomach felt weak. What? Why? How could he say those things? she thought.

"Now I'd like to take Cynthia out to dinner tonight, our last night here, as you know. Can you arrange your schedule to take care of Stephanie? Or do you have other plans? I certainly wouldn't want to interfere with your summer," he said.

"I'll be glad to watch Stephie," A.D. said.

Mr. Cramer put his hands on his hips and stared at her. "You're damn right you'll watch her," he said.

Chapter Twenty-One

"Oh, Rod, it was awful," A.D. said. They were drinking Pepsis at the outdoor restaurant in Harbor Square on Straight Wharf. Stephanie played on the bandstand in front of the place.

"No one has ever yelled at me like that or said such awful, untrue things. He was positively mean."

"Just try and forget it."

"I can't. He makes me feel so rotten. I know I'm not. But he's so convinced I am that I almost believe it too."

"Come on. I'm going to cheer you up. No more talk of Old Man Cramer." Rod crossed his eyes and stuck out his tongue. "You're out with a handsome guy, just think of that."

She had to smile.

"Look, Rod, Stephie's found a little girl friend. They're dancing together. Isn't that cute?"

"I wish you weren't going home tomorrow."

"You have another week yet."

"Yes, but it won't be the same without you."

A.D. blushed. "I'll miss you too, Rod. It's been fun this summer. I won't forget it."

"Hey, let's walk up and get some ice cream. I'm hungry."

"Okay. I'll collect Stephie. She probably won't want to leave now that she's found a friend. Gee, where'd they go?"

A.D. grabbed her tote bag and ran to the bandstand. "Stephie!" she called. "Where are you hiding?"

She saw the little girl Stephie had been dancing with. She was sitting alone on the steps.

"Little girl, where did your friend go?"

The little girl got up and ran.

"Oh, darn. Oh, Stephie," A.D. said.

Rod walked to the bandstand.

"Rod! She just disappeared! I can't see her anywhere!"

"Take it easy," he said. "Now we just saw her. She couldn't have gone far. Don't panic. We'll find her."

A.D. felt ill. Mr. Cramer's angry face kept appearing in her mind. "Oh, God," she pleaded, "where is Stephie? Stephie!"

"Stephie!" Rod called.

A.D. ran to a couple who were coming out of the candy shop. "I've lost a little girl. She has short brown hair. She's wearing a red pants suit. She's two and a half."

The man and woman smiled and said they were sorry but they had not seen the little girl. "I hope she doesn't go near the boats," the man warned.

"Oh, my gosh. Oh, Rod," A.D. called. "We better

look by the anchor on the wharf. You know she loves to see the boats."

"All right, A.D., you go up that way. I'll look around here and behind the shops."

A.D. raced up the street toward the anchor.

"Stephie!"

She kept stopping people to ask if Stephie had come that way. No one had seen her.

As she ran on the boards, nervous sea gulls bent their wings and soared upward, some perching on boat masts and cabin tops, others flying over her head erratically.

"Stephie!" she called hopefully, breathlessly, desperation showing in the tone.

"Have you seen . . . ?" she asked everyone.

"No" was always the answer. Some people offered to help and began looking with her.

Again she called, "Stephie! Stephie!"

She was out of breath. Her pulse beat in her throat. "Oh, my gosh," she cried. "What am I going to do?"

Everything in her wanted to collapse and melt away through the boards. But she had to find Stephie. She *had* to.

Her tote bag was like a great weight on her arm. But still she clung to it. It was good to hold on to something.

"Stephie." She could hear Rod calling now. He was catching up with her. She was glad to see him, but it meant he hadn't found Stephie in the shops by the bandstand.

"Rod, oh, Rod, I'm so scared."

He put his arm behind her back to help her run.

"Let's go this way," he said, leading her toward the docks where some big yachts were moored.

Then they saw her, a tiny figure, standing in front of the last piling on the long pier, behind her the open sea.

A.D. stopped. "Oh, God, how did she get way out there?"

"Let's go slow now," Rod said. "We don't want to frighten her. The water is deep out there."

A.D. prayed silently as they walked toward Stephanie. She held out her arms "Come here, honey," she begged.

Stephanie did not move.

A.D. smiled. "Come on, Stephie. It's time to go home."

"No," the little girl said.

"Let's go get some ice cream, Stephie," Rod said.

"No."

"Why, Stephie? Why won't you come?" A.D. pleaded.

"I go swim."

"No!" A.D. said quickly. She felt Rod move beside her. "Rod, what are you doing?" she whispered.

"I'm going down this ladder here. I'll crawl under the pier and come up behind her."

"But what if—? Rod! You can't swim."

"I'm going," he said.

"Wait." A.D. took a few steps toward Stephanie.

"Don't come, A.D.," the little girl said. "I go swim."

"Oh, Stephie, no. Don't go swim. A.D. loves you. The water is too deep for you, Stephie."

"I can *too* swim," Stephanie said, stamping her foot.

"Keep her talking," Rod whispered. "I'm going under the pier."

"Rod, no! I—oh, wait—let me try something." A.D. kept her eyes on Stephanie while her hands felt in the tote bag. She touched Dorothy and pulled her out.

"Stephie, look, Stephie. It's Dorothy. Hi, Dorothy! Do you see Stephie? What would you like me to tell Stephie?" A.D. put the doll up by her ear.

Stephanie watched her silently.

"Dorothy says she wants you to come and get her. She wants to be *your* baby, Stephie."

The little girl looked surprised.

"Yes, she says she is tired of old A.D. She wants you to be her mother. She wants to belong to *you*, Stephie."

"My baby?" Stephie asked.

"Yes. Come get your baby."

Stephanie ran to A.D. and took Dorothy. She hugged the doll and A.D. hugged Stephanie. She looked at Rod as the tears began. "Oh, Rod, I love this little kid. I really love her."

Rod picked Stephanie up in his arms, and they walked off the pier. Several people who had been helping to look smiled and clapped as they walked by. Rod and A.D. thanked them.

"My baby. My baby now," Stephanie said.

A.D. couldn't stop crying, even when Stephie was back in the stroller and they had had their ice cream and were on the way home.

"I don't care what you think," she told Rod, "I don't care if you think I'm the biggest dope in the world. We found Stephie and I lost Dorothy, and I warn you

116

—I know what you're thinking. Just don't you dare say anything."

"Gosh. I wasn't going to say anything."

"Well, the last thing I need is to be teased about carrying a doll around in my tote."

"I didn't say *anything*."

"Well, why didn't you? It's a pretty dumb thing to be carrying around when you're almost fourteen."

"Gee, I was just thinking that when I got home I was going to send you something in the mail. There's these two ship models I made. They're twin battleships. I guess I made them when I was about eight. They sit on my windowsill at home. I was just thinking I'd send you one of them. I mean, I guess a gray battleship won't mean much to a girl, but I'd like you to have one if you'd want one."

"Oh, Rod. That's the nicest thing. . . ." She couldn't finish because a new flood of tears fell from her eyes.

Chapter Twenty-Two

That night, her last in the beautiful old Nantucket bedroom, a knock on A.D.'s door wakened her. She was frightened.

"Who's there?" she called.

"Mr. Cramer. Don't open the door. Just come stand by it so you can hear me. I don't want to shout."

A.D. put on her robe. "It's okay. I can open the door."

"No," he said quickly. "I'll talk through the door. I—well, uh, Cynthia and I had a little talk tonight, and I know now I shouldn't have said those things to you today. I had no idea things were as bad as that with any wife. I mean I knew that she got a little depressed now and then, but, well, Cynthia told me about this summer and how much you helped her. She said you did *everything*. I feel like the biggest fool. I kept hoping it was a phase she would get through. Now I know better. She's sick. She needs help, professional help, and I'm going to get it for her when we get home. She's going right to the doctor. I just wanted you to know. Are you still there?"

"Yes. Okay. I'm glad. I'm sure she'll be fine real soon. I really like her."

"I should have spent more time here this summer. I work too much. But at my company, if you take a vacation, you might come back and find someone else sitting at your desk. Well, you'd better get back to sleep. We leave on the second boat tomorrow. I was upset this afternoon. Do you understand?"

"It's okay," A.D. said. She knew how awful it must be for Mr. Cramer to admit he was wrong. She knew why he had to say it through a closed door. He had probably never admitted being wrong before.

She waited until she heard Mr. Cramer go back to his room, then she opened her door and went to check on Stephanie, shivering when she thought of her standing on the long pier.

A.D. held on to the crib rail and looked down at the sleeping child. Dorothy was lying on the baby pillow, staring up at the ceiling. A.D. reached out and closed the doll's eyes.

"Oh, Dorothy, we've had quite a summer, haven't we? You take care of Stephie now, hear?"

She tiptoed back to her bed and went to sleep.

The next morning Rod came by early and helped Mr. Cramer load the station wagon. Harold Poopsie barked at them as they worked. A.D. served everyone breakfast, then washed the dishes and packed the last box of kitchen staples. Mrs. Cramer walked through each room saying good-bye to the old house.

"We'll be back again," she said, "maybe not next summer, but we will be back. Have you spoken to the caretaker, Jerry?" she asked.

"Yes," Mr. Cramer said. "He'll make sure about the water pipes and locking up."

"Well, then . . ." she said.

"Yes. It's time to go home."

Rod rode down to the wharf with them. Their car was first in line for loading.

Mrs. Cramer said, "A.D., you don't have to wait in the car. Here's your ticket. You and Rod can say good-bye, and you can go up the passenger ramp. When the boat sails, we'll meet you on the top deck." She handed A.D. her boarding ticket.

Rod and A.D. got out of the car. Rod said good-bye to the Cramers and to Stephanie. He and A.D. walked over to the dock to look for the boat.

"Rod, your face is red," A.D. teased.

"Yeah, well, you'll blush too when I sweep you into my arms in a dramatic good-bye."

A.D. giggled.

"You think I won't?" he said.

"What?"

"Kiss you good-bye." He said it softly, seriously.

A.D. gulped and looked away from him. She couldn't think of anything to say. The ferry steamer came into sight.

"There's the boat," Rod said.

A.D. nodded.

"It was a good summer, wasn't it?" he said.

She nodded again, and her face became all screwed up in a funny way.

"Hey, you're not going to be dopey and cry all over me, are you?"

She burst out laughing and crying at the same time. "I might. I'm pretty dopey."

They saw the ferry steamer move into Nantucket Harbor.

"I'll write," Rod said.

"Okay. I'll write too."

"Well, here goes," he said. He took hold of her shoulders and moved his face toward hers.

The boat's whistle blasted. They both jumped, and his kiss landed on her right eye.

"Ouch!" she said, cupping her hand over it but laughing too.

Rod smiled. "Gee, I think I could use a little practice. We should have started this hugging and kissing stuff earlier."

The big boat docked, and the passengers came down the ramp. When the cars began to move onto the pier, the Cramer's car was the first to be driven on.

"Well, I'd better get on board."

"Yes. So long. I'll write."

"Me too."

A.D. walked up the ramp. "I'll wave to you from the second deck. Look for me," she called.

In a few minutes she knew he had spotted her. She waved and he waved, and the ferry steamer moved away from the dock and toward the mainland.

A.D. watched Rod grow smaller until she couldn't

see him at all. Then the dock grew smaller and soon she could no longer see Jetties Beach. Suddenly there was nothing, nothing but water. Nantucket was gone like a dream. She watched the gray-and-white sea gulls flapping after the ship. It's over, she thought, my beautiful summer is over.

She turned to go to the top deck to look for the Cramers. Again she cupped her hand over her right eye. It was still sore. Wow, what a powerful kisser, she thought.